Unhinged

A Novel by Sierra Kay

2011 The Vega Group LLC Paperback Edition

Unhinged
Sierra Kay

This book is dedicated to those who catch me when I fall and those who encourage me to move forward when I stand still. I love you all.

Thank you.

Shelia

2003

Shelia Cordell-Sims slipped her narrow five-foot-three frame into the oak chair, hooked her feet around the front legs, and laid the side of her honey-kissed face on the oak table warmed by the early afternoon sun. She made circular motions with her hand following the table grain.

There wasn't a nick or a scratch on the table. Not one man-made imperfection—only the subtle variations of the natural wood. But even these imperfections were just … what … just perfect.

The tapping of the sheer curtains against the window frame beckoned her. She drug her body out of the chair, across her cherrywood floor to the living room window. Viewing her nearly empty street, she watched the harried nanny walking five-year-old Kendall down the street. Shelia was sure Kendall was putting the nanny in her place about something. Disney spends big money convincing little girls that they should be princesses and from what Shelia observed during the past month, Kendall was gunning for the position of the queen.

Shelia felt a smile tug at her lips and caressed her empty womb with her hand. The caress turned into a grab at the top of her pristine, well-pressed, white linen shorts. She took a deep breath, closed her eyes, and exhaled gently.

She glanced at her white gym shoes lined up by the door. She yearned to run outside, throw her hands up, spinning in circles until she was too dizzy to do anything but drop on the grass, laugh, and let the sunshine warm her directly instead of through the table.

She tugged her linen blouse out of the confining waist of her shorts and opened the second button. Her wedding band was cutting off the circulation in her finger. Everything felt so tight all of a sudden.

Walking through the kitchen, she opened a bag of popcorn, ate a handful, folded the top neatly and applied the 'chip clip.' She picked up the phone to call Zelphia, but slowly depressed the call button.

Zel needed answers and Shelia still had none. Zel wouldn't wait forever. Soon she'd come beating down Shelia's door. She had been more patient than Shelia ever thought possible. The real Zel would come clawing out like a wildebeest soon enough.

Zel was the kind of friend who proved that whether or not the grass was greener on the other side was irrelevant. Her argument was who cares if it's not greener, at least it's different than the side you were on. At least that was the Zel she knew once.

Mother didn't really approve of Zel. Just thinking of Mother brought a snort of incredulity that she was born of that woman. She had tried for years to call Mother other names—mommy, mom, ma. Missy Cordell was Mother.

Mother approved of Zel's bank balance and her contacts. Mother wouldn't offend Zel and give up all those fancy parties to which Zel got her tickets or those fancy clothes Zel made for her. But she despised her with a deep-seated simmering urgency that would never boil, but it also would never be quite cool. Even when she smiled and laughed with Zel, her disdain was evident both in her posture and in her eyes.

Zel always had questions and thinly veiled demands. She always wanted more for everyone. Shelia was often just too tired to deflect her barrage, so she seldom called.

As college roommates, it was great. It was new and exciting. Shelia rode the Zel wave and had a great time. Then, life happened for both of them. Their relationship had never been quite the same. Those lies that they told themselves and each other had damaged something precious.

Every conversation since then was tinged with a bit of betrayal and a hint of mistrust. It was more like constantly walking on broken glass. Your feet get tough, but you still hear the distinct cracking with each step.

Shelia made herself a promise. She wasn't hiding anymore. That even meant talking to Zel when she didn't have any good excuse to cut the call short. So she took a deep breath, pressed the call button and dialed a lengthy set of international numbers to call Zel in Paris.

"Hey, Zel."

"Shelia? What the hell? I've been trying to reach you. You know the job offer is still open. But damn, if you don't want it, just say so. It's better than pulling the smoke move. Shit, you disappear better than a cheating husband."

Shelia smiled. "I don't know what I'm going to do yet. I just … I didn't want to disappoint you. I didn't know what to tell you, but I'm trying to do better. That's my deal with myself. I'm going to do better in a lot of ways."

Zel sounded skeptical."Yeah, OK. What's going on? Are you pregnant? Did you give in to that frozen fish of a husband? "

Shelia rolled her eyes. "No, I'm not pregnant. And don't call him that. He's the one footing the bills around here."

"You could find a job. I offered you one. That's on you. What are you trying to do better with?"

Shrugging, Shelia said"I don't know. Life, maybe. I realized I kinda checked out years ago."

"That's not a news flash. So what's making you check back in?"

"I don't like me. That's a horrible place to be. I don't like how I look. I don't like that I rarely laugh anymore. I used to laugh. I remember. I used to laugh a lot. I can't seem to get myself together enough to do anything, but sweep, mop, and make beds. I used to be smart. I used to be able to think. I don't think that I've thought in years. How about that?"

Zelphia paused. "Are you seeing a shrink?"

"No, I'm not seeing a shrink."

"So, this revelation …?"

"It's just time. I'm too old and too young to be this … person. It's hard to explain."

Zelphia agreed. "I told you that years ago. I told you that on your wedding day."

"Really, I'm trying to talk to you and the best you have is that you told me so? For real?"

"Fine. I'll be the understanding friend. I'm happy that you came to that realization. I'm glad you're on the right track. I'm just still not sure what brought all this on. There just seems to be more than 'it's time.' I feel like I've read the beginning and the end, but I completely missed the middle. So what does it mean that you want to do better?"

Shelia let out a small, self-deprecating laugh. "I have no idea. But can I reserve the right, now, to tell you when I figure it out? I may just need a shrink to sort this through. I have literally been getting less and less comfortable in my own skin. I'm anxious. I can't live like this. So I'm going to start with one thing at a time. The first thing is reaching out to my very best friend, and tell her I'm going to change; that I love her and that I don't think she knows how much of a lifeline she's been. Step one. A baby step, but I think it's necessary."

"Ah, Baby Girl."

"No, no jokes. Don't brush it aside. Just say thank you."

"Thank you."

"And I will call you later. I'm not ducking you anymore. Just say OK."

"OK."

"Talk to you later." Shelia smiled. That wasn't all that bad. She knew once the shock wore off, Zel was going to call her back with a number of questions. She'd deal with that when the time came. Hopefully, she'd find answers. This revelation came as a shock to her, too.

Her step two was going to be a doozy. She had to come to terms with why she checked out. She didn't need a shrink to tell her that she needed to figure out a way to deal with the fact that more than five years earlier she'd given her daughter to two complete strangers to raise, crossed her fingers, hoping for the best. Every day since, she'd paid for that decision. Right or wrong, it was her call to make. Now, she was going to have to learn to live with it.

She knew, without a doubt, having another baby with her husband, Devon Sims, was not going to be the cure. She had to do this now, before she could begin to deal with what he thought she was already trying to do—get pregnant.

Had Shelia been raised in a normal home, this wouldn't have been a big deal. People get pregnant every single day. No muss, no fuss. Single moms are all over the place. They make it work. Hell, Shelia herself was raised by a single mom. However, she was told, taught, forced to believe that she had to be more, better. It was drilled into her on a daily basis, sometimes multiple times.

This was, of course, because Shelia's father was broke and absent. The government didn't know where or if he worked, so child support was nonexistent. That and the fact that he was busy populating the world. She had lost count of her half-siblings. To this day, they were still popping up. His ass was way too old for that craziness.

Yet, Mother still believed in being supported by a man. She lived in a world of traditional roles, where a wife could stay home and the husband "brought home the bacon." Mother believed she just settled for love; she wasn't pragmatic enough. Now Mother was more than pragmatic; she was coldly focused and determined.

Mother's goals now were for Shelia and centered on a big house and wealthy husband, who could support her in the way to which Mother felt she was born to be, but never quite achieved. Happiness wasn't even a footnote in the equation. Love? Shit, love was for books. It was for bedtime stories. Real life was completely different. "You can't raise kids on love alone. How do you expect them to eat?"

Mother had tried by making sure Shelia went to the best private schools. It didn't matter that the school was an hour and a half from the house. It was the best. She was convinced that the school she chose would help introduce Shelia to the upper crust of society and help Shelia find a good—meaning "rich"—husband.

But the boys from the private schools weren't hanging around after graduation to marry the girl next door. They definitely weren't trying to hookup with shy Shelia. Well, that's not quite true. They tried to hook up with anything in a skirt, but they weren't offering rings. They rarely called most girls the next day. If the girls weren't with the game, the guys moved on down the line. They kept that train moving all the way to college.

So Mother decided to send Shelia in the same direction. While they could scrape together private high school tuition, private college tuition was a different matter. A lot had to be done with partial scholarships and student loans. Eventually, Shelia ended up at Carlington University.

1997

The first day was the first glimpse of what Shelia's life could be. Mother was drilling the already harried resident assistant about the limitations on male visitations in an all-girls dorm. She wanted to make sure there were limited opportunities for assaults on Shelia's virtue. Swear to God,the fact that this was the late 1990s passed right by.

Shelia zoned Mother out, ignored the desperate plea in the eyes of the resident assistant, and stared out of the window. Everyone was carrying boxes, laughing, and chatting.

Shelia had her opportunities pounded into her head repeatedly. Mother had spent hours detailing her responsibility for the future of the family: find a rich man. However, the girls filling the rooms down the hall with boxes, had lighter steps than the one dragging the weight of familial responsibility.

The resident assistant was easing her way out of the room with a lot of, "Umm hmm. I'm sure Shelia will be fine. Yes, I'll definitely keep an eye on her. No one would dare sneak boys in this dorm. Yes. I understand your concern. Umm, hmm. I do have other residents to tend to. Of course, answers to your questions are important. Umm, hmm …"

Just then a breeze from outside blew in, breaking the stress. She was five-feet-eleven, at least, even without her three-inch heels. She had highlighted hair and wore jeans and an orange top that would scream at anyone from across the quad.

Shelia was amazed. This wasn't just stature. This was presence.

She was carrying a box that she quickly dropped on the empty bed closest to the door.

"Hi, Mrs. Cordell; and you must be Shelia."

Mother looked the new girl up and down, and in her best princess-to-pauper voice said, "It's Ms. Am I supposed to know you?"

"Forgive me. I cheated a bit and peaked at the room assignment list in the reception area. I'm Zelphia, or Zel. Either one will do. I'm not too picky."

The resident assistant had conveniently slipped out the minute Zel arrived.

There was laughter in Zel's eyes as she stressed the correct pronunciation. "*Mz.* Cordell. Those are wicked shoes. Do you mind me asking where you got them?"

Preening, Shelia's mother looked down at her strappy black patent leather sandals with three-inch heels. "Oh these? Just a little boutique in Chicago." Mother always used the boutique line to make her clothing seem a bit more exotic and a bit less average.

"Really! My mom is Tyla Shaw of Designs by Tyla. You may have heard of her. She has a boutique in Chicago."

"Of course. She designs clothing for local celebrities as well as some people in New York and LA. Wasn't she just featured in *Today's Chicago Woman*?"

"That's her, all right. She had a show, or she would have come up with me–but if Shelia's open to giving a hand to a poor college student, we can get my stuff up in no time at all and get settled in. I'd really like to get everything set up tonight. I'm the queen of procrastination. If I don't do it now, I'll still have boxes in my trunk for the next three weeks."

Zel looked around the room. "I see you have all of your stuff in its place. Wow, did y'all get here at dawn? So, Mz. Cordell, are you staying down tonight or are you driving home?"

The question was purely innocent. The tilt of Zel's head was purely inquisitive. The constant twinkle in Zel's eyes was not.

"I'm planning on driving home."

"Well, it was nice meeting you. Shelia, when you're ready to give a hand, I'm driving the red 1970s Trans Am with the eagle on the hood in the first row of the parking lot. Can't miss me," Zel said, and breezed out of the room.

"Aren't you fortunate to room with someone with such good contacts? So exciting. I hope you'll get to meet some decent people.

I'll give you a call when I get home," Mother said as she, too, headed out.

Shelia sat on the bed and took her first free breath. Her breathing relaxed with each step her mother took down the hall. She waited a full five minutes before moving. Then, giggling, she ran down to help Zel with her stuff, feeling pounds lighter than when she dragged her belongings into the room.

AYAAN

2003

Ayaan Travers watched her daughter, Kendall, drag Cleo, the nanny, down the street. The park was a huge deal to Kendall, and she didn't want to waste a minute getting there. Even worse for the nanny, but the absolute best for Kendall, they were going to have a picnic, complete with a basket of fried chicken left over from last night's dinner.

Ayaan's full lips thinned into a smile. She tucked the left side of her shoulder-length bob behind her ear. Moving away from the window, she started to head for the home office. She was wearing her usual home office attire, black jeans and a button-up blouse. She felt more comfortable dressed for work, even if she didn't have to leave the house.

She was fortunate that her website consulting business had afforded her two notable perks. One was the ability to work from home. The second was enough money to afford full-time help with Kendall. She was able to see Kendall during the day, but still have time to dedicate to her work.

The business was doing exceptionally well. In fact, it had reached a point where she had to turn down business. That was crazy to her. She had spent the first three years clawing her way to get some steady business. Now, she worked for a few advertising agencies that recognized the need to branch out into website design, but didn't want to staff it yet. She filled the gap. She could show up at presentations but, for the most part, stayed in the background doing the work. This work didn't require her to be in the office all that much. She could work while Cleo was watching Kendall or late at night.

She walked away from the window and headed to the recently remodeled kitchen to brew a cup of tea. She would prefer tea and a slice of cake. While she wasn't a fanatic about her size or her weight, she had made herself a promise that she would never have to shop at Lane Bryant or Ashley Stewart. So when her weight crept up, she skipped the snacks.

Every time she came into the kitchen, she admired her designer's work. The kitchen was upgraded to stainless steel appliances and cool perks she had yet to use—like a warming drawer and pot filler; most of the time she forgot they were there. She had given her designer almost carte blanche to create a space that would lift it from the tired kitchen that the house had when she moved in four years ago to a show space.

This, too, was purchased with her own money. Truth be told, she made out like a bandit in the divorce. Ayaan had needed that money when she found herself divorced with a newborn child. Soon she found the stride she had before she poured everything into what she was building with Kenneth.

The divorce always caused her to pause. She had waited forever for love. When they met, she was thirty-four and he was twenty-nine.

At six-feet-one, he was the way she liked her men—tall, slender, six-packed chocolate king with a naughty smile.

Theoretically, she wanted to get married; however, she wasn't as desperate as many people thought. They had started talking about her ticking biological clock, but the batteries had run out on that years ago. She was happy. She didn't hear the clock.

Kenneth fit into the chocolate mold, and if his reputation was well-deserved, he was also a bad boy. The first thing he did wasn't hit on her; he made her laugh. It wasn't even a cute, fake-date laugh. It was a gut-busting, open-mouthed, can't-catcha-breath, need-an-oxygen-mask laugh. He had women swarming, and Ayaan had men promising forever. So for them, friendship fit well.

They had mutual friends, which placed them around each other a lot. There wasn't any drama because they didn't date. She didn't care about what he did or with whom. He didn't say a word when they were out to dinner, and she would get a call then suddenly jet for the door. They were *friends* first.

At the time, Ayaan was working at a public relations firm, while Kenneth was a freelance writer and actor. She was working on a small freelance project of her own, doing media training for a friend that ran a not-for-profit. He was being interviewed on Channel 9 and was a bit nervous in front of the television camera. To complete the training, she needed someone with a video camera. Kenneth fit the bill. It also helped that some of his acting techniques worked well for her client. Chicago Lights Camera Action was born to help businesspeople become camera-ready. Business *partners* second.

Three years into their business and friendship, they were out celebrating a particularly nice paycheck. The next part was so out of character that, to this day, Ayaan blames it on the amount of alcohol she drank.

She looked up at Kenneth and felt a tightening in her stomach that she swore hadn't been there before. She realized that everything she wanted in a man, everything she hadn't been able to find had been there. His bottom lip was calling to her. She did something she had never done—made the first move. She leaned over and kissed him, right on the side of his lips. He looked at her like she'd lost her mind.

If she was going to make a move on her best friend and potentially lose him in the process, it needed to be a move that at least represented her skills. So she leaned in again. She loved the art of the kiss. While he was surprised at first, he was also a quick study.

They became *lovers* third and *married* when she was thirty-eight.

Shelia

2003

The ringing phone jerked Shelia back to the present. Instinct had her reaching for it automatically before caution caught up and made her check the caller ID. Mother. She stared at the phone as she stepped slowly back. Eventually the ringing ceased. Two minutes later it began again. If Mother was anything, she was predictable. Her messages were always two and three calls; –but while voice mail can relay the message, it's not the same as the voice of a daughter. Mother would call back later.

Her commitment to change and to do better in her friendships did not extend to Mother yet. Their relationship had always been strained; her mother called her a surprise. What shouldn't have been a surprise was how bootlegged her father was. This man hadn't supported any child that he'd fathered. By the time Shelia was born, he'd worked his way up to a soccer team. Now, he might be on a full gospel choir. Shelia had lost count. All she knew was that he never kept a job long enough for the Department of Children and Family

Services to catch up with him to garnish a check.

Missy Cordell was the force, the will, the forty-five-year-old Kendall. Her mother had never met Sheila's neighbor, Kendall. They probably couldn't be in the same room together. Their wills were too strong. Two queens couldn't rule one kingdom. Sharing wasn't an option for strong personalities. Dominance was.

It was that need to dominate which caused Mother to try to convince herself that Shelia's father could change. He could keep a job. He could be a good father. He could stop populating the world. Yeah, that didn't quite work out the way Missy had intended.

So Missy kicked him out of her orbit and controlled every other aspect of her life. Ever since Shelia was young, the sun rose and set on Mother. Her friends always thought that she had to be spoiled, because she was an only child. But such was not the case; her mother's needs always came first, under the guise that everything she did, she did for both of them.

1990

Shelia remembered the time when, as president of the student council, she was going to speak in front of her school's Parent's Club. She was president because none of the "cool" kids wanted the designation, but also because that's what Mother wanted. You can't brag about your child's accomplishments if she hasn't accomplishing anything. As nerdy as it was, Shelia was still excited. This was the biggest thing in her eleven-year-old life.

Her mother was supposed to come home with new shoes to go with the suit that Shelia was to wear. However, new shoes took the backseat to the new dress Mother had to have for the meeting. Mother figured Shelia's old shoes were good enough. Not a big deal really, but it was Shelia's night, her time to shine.

Yeah, she shined, shined her old shoes so they looked halfway decent with the suit. Shelia still looked nice, and Mother, as always, looked beautiful. Stylish. Looked like she could substantiate the lies she told about her age. Shelia should have learned then that even when it was about her, it was never *really* about her–but Shelia held out hope. She wanted to think the best—that underneath it all, Mother really had her daughter's best interest at heart. Mothers were supposed to— naturally; but Shelia learned that nature only goes so far, as Mother proved once again when it came to an important school project. She remembered it vividly.

"Shelia, darling. Come on down."

"Yes, Mother."

"You wouldn't believe what happened to me today at work. The company bought a block of tickets to a benefit feature—none other than the Alvin Ailey dance troupe. My boss reserved two tickets. Can you believe it? Some of partners will be there. I think I'll wear that cream number in my closet."

"What about my science project? It's due tomorrow. You didn't have time to take me to the store yesterday or the day before. First it was the dinner where your company bought the table. Then you had to go clothes shopping for your trip this weekend. I ran out of supplies, and I need to finish up."

Mother turned and raised one eyebrow. "You think I'm doing this for myself? That I wouldn't rather help you? I need contacts to move up, and I'm just not getting the right ones at work."

"Mother, if I don't do the science project, I'll fail."

"Excuse me. I don't think I heard you right. Cordell's don't fail. We haven't yet, and we won't.

"But Mother—"

"You've had the project for a month, and you waited until the last minute to finish it. Matter of fact, I think I should suspend your television privileges for the weekend. You had plenty of time, instead of waiting until the last minute. Now I'm supposed to drop everything?"

"No, Mother."

"I'll get Stephie's mother to take you to the store. I'm sure her calendar is empty. All she has to do all day is aerobics, seeing as how Steve pays for everything. In case you didn't notice, I'm alone out here, and it's hard. I'd appreciate a little sympathy instead of attitude."

"Who's staying with me?"

"What?"

"I'm eleven, Mother. I can't stay here by myself. "

"Of course not. You're staying at Stephie's and going to school from there tomorrow. I talked to her mother from work and everything is arranged. Now, I've got to go change."

With that, Mother left to hobnob with the bosses. Of course, it never got her the promotion she was constantly campaigning for, but she did get to see one of the best concert performances in the city.

She used to say, "No date can ever take me the places I'm going with this company." Actually, all the kissing up only got her as far as the senior administrative assistant over all the other "admins," but you'd never know it by Mother's attitude. Fifteen years later, she's still all fake flash.

2003

Shelia opened the back door and surveyed her garden— sheltered from prying eyes by a high wood fence and foliage. Some of it had sprouted on its own. She wanted the wildflowers. Bully for them, if they could survive and flourish, if they could break their way in and demand a spot in the sun. What right did she have to kill that spirit? Shelia walked over to the wild grass and breathed in the smell of the wildflowers. She smiled fully, showing her slightly crooked front tooth.

Devon didn't know the difference; he just pretended that he did. At first, he wanted to take those out. He thought the garden should be sculpted. So Shelia lied to him; she told him the landscaper did it. It was just a little lie, but it made her feel better; and as long as the landscaper said it was fine, it was fine with Devon.

Shelia was so comfortable with people who pretended to be more than they were, that she actually married someone just like Mother.

Devon was a lawyer at the law firm where Mother worked. He was five-feet-five, a bit round and a bit bald. He was also a bit mean. He wasn't abusive. He just didn't really care about other people's feelings,

Last night, they had a rare argument; most of the time they spent as roommates. However, lately Shelia had been so focused on herself that she hadn't picked up his dry cleaning. Devon didn't like that at all. He wanted to wear his power suit combination for a meeting, and it wasn't in their closet.

"Shelia, why isn't my suit in the closet?"

Shelia let out a mental "F" bomb. "Which suit? You have a closet full."

"The suit that I specifically asked you to take to the dry cleaners so that I could wear it tomorrow. The only custom-made suit that I own. You know the one with the custom-made shirt. The only one I ever ask for specifically."

"Yeah. It's, um, at the cleaners."

"Why?

"Because I forgot to pick it up."

Shelia could see him struggling internally to keep his temper in check. "What the fuck else do you have to do around here? Your only job is to take care of the goddamn house. Part of that is making sure the one damn suit that I ask you to have cleaned actually makes it out of the cleaners."

Sheila didn't say anything. It was rare for him to care this much about anything.

"I don't ask you for anything. You don't care about my job. OK. You don't ask me how my day was. Fine. Sex is nonexistent. I deal with it. You are getting skinnier by the minute, so holding you is like sleeping with a stick figure. Whatever. So all this marriage shit is fucked. The least you can do is ensure anything at all that touches my career stays on point. That is non-negotiable. You can walk around here like a zombie on crack, but you better support my work."

"You'll have it before you go to work tomorrow," Sheila said. As she left the bedroom, she heard Devon throwing things around the room. He'd called her a zombie on crack. She hadn't seen that temper before, but she couldn't really blame him. They had only had sex twice since they had moved into this house about a month ago. As average as her husband was in all things social, he was damn near phenomenal and a bit insatiable in bed. A month after the move, she was still claiming fatigue, but her time was running out.

She made a mental note to get up early in the morning and high-tail it to the cleaners to get his suit before he got out of the shower in the morning. No need to make a bad situation worse.

Before, she at least pretended to be engaged for the two to three hours a day that they had together after he got home from work. They would sit down to eat and make small talk. Sometimes, they would watch a movie, unless he had a case to work on—which meant he would return to the office and work. Now, she wasn't even managing that after-work support.

Devon was driven by results. Like Shelia, he didn't start out with advantages, but he had drive and ambition. He had worked for years and saved the money to go to law school full-time without working or taking out student loans. He finally enrolled when he turned thirty-two. He decided when he was thirty-seven that he wanted to get married.

Mother introduced them, and they got along well. It wasn't love, but it would do. He had done a great job winning cases and working his way up. His reputation as a lawyer kept growing. They originally lived in Chicago; but as he got serious about this baby business, he wanted to be close to good schools. Now, they were out in the suburb of Flossmoor. He wasn't too excited about living in the south suburbs; the property values didn't rise very quickly. This was Shelia's choice. On this, she was non-negotiable.

AYAAN

2003

Ayaan had gotten quite a bit of work done while Kendall was at the park. It was suddenly interrupted by a loud yell that made her jump.

"Mommy, we're home from the picnic. I saved you a piece of chicken. Mommy!"

Ayaan heard Cleo trying to hush Kendall. "Remember Kendall, when mommy is working, we have to wait until she's done."

"But she'd want to know that I'm back."

"OK, sweetie. I'm sure she knows now."

"But, she'd want to see me."

"Tell you what. Why don't we make a note to slip under her office door? That way she'll know that you're home. OK? We can practice your letters."

Ayaan heard Kendall running to her playroom before she heard her shout, "I'll get the paper."

Ayaan would have loved to have opened the door the minute she heard Kendall's voice. It was all she could do not to get a hug from Kendall. However, she was working hard to get Kendall to respect the closed-office-door policy. It was usually Ayaan who backtracked first, so Ayaan and Cleo came up with the note system.

Kendall loved it, because Ayaan hung her notes on the bulletin board. Ayaan wasn't disturbed during her work day—not by much anyway. The truth was, for the last month she'd been having a hard time with separation from Kendall. That was probably the hardest part of working at home. When Kendall wasn't at her three-day-a-week kindergarten, it was so hard for Ayaan to concentrate on her work. Kendall was more than a handful. She was full of energy and opinions. She could be exhausting, but Ayaan couldn't imagine her daughter any other way.

Ayaan hung out in the office fifteen minutes after Cleo and Kendall slipped the note under the door, and then she joined them in the playroom.

"Mommy, I'm doing my homework."

"So, I see. It looks like you're doing a good job."

"Yup. See I'm taking my time so the letters are perfect."

"I see. How was the park?"

"Ohh, it was great!"

Kendall told her mother about the boy that ate sand. Kendall laughed. "He's so silly. People don't eat sand. He can't come to my birthday party eating sand."

Ayaan looked at Cleo who just shrugged her shoulders.

"Kendall, do we know the little boy who likes to eat sand?"

"No, but I want everyone to come to my party."

"Yes, I know dear, but you remember when we had the conversation about invitations and giving people advance notice."

Kendall let out a huge sigh. "I know, but it will be fun. Everyone should have fun. And I didn't invite him. He eats sand."

Ayaan knew her daughter very well. She tended to leave out pertinent details. She may not have invited the sand-eating boy, but she probably did invite some other children at the park. This party was getting to be out of hand. "Sweetie, did you invite other people at the park?"

"Yup, there was a little girl. She was a baby. She didn't talk real good. So I told her mommy about my party."

Ayaan looked over at Cleo, who merely shrugged again. They both knew stopping Kendall was like corralling a tornado.

"Do I know her mother?"

"I don't know."

"Does she know where you live?"

"I couldn't give my address. You told me not to give our address and phone number to strangers anymore. So I just told them which house."

"Is there anyone else that might come to the party?"

"Well, just people from school. And the sad lady next door."

Ayaan sat up straight. "Why the sad lady from next door?"

"She was going to her mailbox and didn't say hi. I showed her my curls, and I don't think she liked them. I like them, though."

"Did she say she didn't like them?"

"No, but she looked like she was going to cry. Who cries over curls? I told her that you said that she thinks too much."

Ayaan closed her eyes. This was too much. "Why did you tell her that?"

"It's whatchu said."

"How did she know about your birthday party?"

"I told her that she always walks around with a frown. I told her she should smile. She should come to my birthday party because it'll make her smile. I told her you think she needs to smile more, too."

"What did she say to that?"

"She smiled, but it was a really sad smile. So I told her that I want her to come and that you would want her to come, too, so she wouldn't be so sad. She's a grown-up, so I told her about the invitation, but I didn't have any. So I told her to put it on her calendar like you said Mommy."

"Yeah, that's what I said. Let's make a deal. Why don't you tell me about the people you want to invite to the party before you actually invite them?"

"Why? You said it's good to help people. That anytime I can help, I should."

"True, but we want everyone to have a good time. We have to plan for everything, including food and seats."

"Oh. Yeah, we want people to have cake. We don't want to run out of cake. OK, Mommy." Kendall hopped up and gave Ayaan a hug.

Ayaan gave her daughter a tight squeeze.

"Mommy that hurts."

"How about this?" She began to tickle Kendall, who giggled, shrieked, and wiggled away.

Cleo quietly left the room. She knew she would be off for the rest of the night. If Ayaan needed her, she would just holler up to her room.

The next morning, Cleo took Kendall to school. Ayaan took a deep breath. It was time to visit with the new neighbor.

She walked over next door and rang the bell.

When Shelia answered the door, she didn't look surprised to see her.

"You told me you were moving. You'd think you would have mentioned that you were moving next door to me," Ayaan snapped.

"What would you have done?"

"I don't know—packed up and moved myself. Do my best to talk you out of it. I don't know, but this is too much."

"I'm surprised it took you this long to come over. I thought you'd be knocking on my door the day I moved in."

"Do I get to come in?"

"Of course, yeah. Come on in."

Ayaan led her into the back of the house and out onto the patio. They both sat down and just stared at each other.

Shelia didn't know what she expected. She hadn't really thought about it, but had hoped Ayaan had been doing well. She looked fantastic. Her hair was long and jet black with bangs and long wisps; she was wearing black jeans and a black cotton shirt. Her eyes looked wary; she had every reason to be.

"I'm not trying to get her back."

"Good, because I don't give a fuck that your husband is Devon Sims, new hot shot lawyer on the block."

"You won't have to fight him. He doesn't know that she exists."

Even in her pissed-off state, that penetrated Ayaan's mind and sidetracked her a bit. "What the hell? That's a hell of a secret to keep from the man you married."

"Well, no one here really knows what happened in Paris, which brings up an interesting question. Why are you celebrating Kendall's birthday in June? It's not until December."

Ayaan shrugged. "For her first birthday, I had a party in December at my house. My nerves can't take that again, so I decided we'd celebrate what we call her half birthday. She's five and a half. She gets to have her friends attend. I get to keep them running around outside. My sanity stays intact. It's a win-win. Trust me; but let's get back on topic."

"I always wondered why you wanted an open adoption, and why you were so specific about the parents; but at the time, I was so happy to get her that I didn't care. I wanted her so badly I would have agreed to anything. Photos once a year and the knowledge of where she was seemed like a small price to pay for Kendall. Her birth mother moving in next door is more than I bargained for, however. I've been watching and listening, but you didn't do anything. You didn't even talk to her until yesterday."

Shelia shrugged. "Devon wants a baby. And I haven't told him that I already have a baby. I can't seem to make myself do what it takes to get pregnant. He stopped using condoms, so I started on the pill. We began to look for houses, and he wanted to move to Naperville. I thought, well, since we were moving, why not closer to her?

I never planned to move next door, but the real estate agent found this house. It was one of the few Devon actually liked. I thought it was meant to be. I know I shouldn't have. Deep in my heart, I know it was the worst thing I could have done to you; but at the same time, I couldn't make myself do anything else."

Ayaan looked at Shelia and wanted to scream. Every word was a needle pricking her skin. Ayaan fulfilled her part of the bargain. She did the right thing. She wanted to slap Shelia. She really wanted to just reach across the table and lay her out. For a month she had been thinking of all the things she would say to this woman who had given her the most precious gift and then made a move to destroy her family.

However, being this close to Shelia, as much as she knew in her heart how selfish this move was, she also saw what a toll this had taken on her. Shelia looked worse today than the day after she gave birth, when she handed Kendall over. She was thinner. She was sadder. She was a hot-ass, selfish bitch of a mess.

"When I saw that you moved in, it was everything I could do not to come over. Kenneth always figured you'd try to get her back. I called him ranting and raving. The second person I called was my lawyer."

"I'm not here to break up your home." Shelia looked directly at Ayaan.

Ayaan squinted and pursed her lips.

"You don't believe me. Listen, I—"

"No, I believe that's what you want to believe. Just like you couldn't 'help yourself' when you moved into this house, I don't think you'll be able to 'help yourself' and you'll hurt both Kendall and me."

"Listen, I have held on to this secret for years. Hell, my mother doesn't even know. If I say anything, it won't just be your family that I'll ruin. It'll be my family, too."

"How can you do this?"

"At the time, I didn't know how I couldn't. Now, I don't know how I can. I see her every day. On one hand, it's the hardest thing to not wrap her up in my arms and tell her I'm her mother. Then, I see her skipping around the nanny and hear her laugh. I realize that Kendall is happy. She is truly happy."

"I'm not sure I could have made her that happy. I know that today, I can't make her that happy. At the end of the day, I wanted my daughter to be happy. She is. You've made her that way. I can't take that happiness from her. Regardless of what I may think I want, the truth is her smile both tears me apart and sets me free."

Ayaan got up and pointed at Shelia. "See, see. That's the part I don't trust. What am I supposed to do with the side that tears you apart? I don't want you at her party. Tell her you forgot you had another appointment in your calendar. She understands about appointments. Tell her you're sorry. Stay away from my daughter. If you see her coming, go the other fucking way."

"You're right about one thing. She is happy. She is happy with the only mother she knows. And I swear I will cut you deep before I let you hurt my daughter. You gave her up. I don't know why. I gave you a chance to change your mind. You handed her over to me and told me I was her mother."

"So know this, you can look at her all you want through your window, but don't you dare try to build a friendship or relationship. If I get even a hint, that you are being more than an absentee neighbor, I will do everything in my power to take you down. Nothing will save you from Kendall's pissed-off mother. Trust that."

With that, Ayaan turned and went out the front door. She should go home, but instead she decided to walk around the block. She needed air. She needed to punch something. It probably should have been Shelia. That might have made her feel better. She couldn't believe this shit. She had to move into that house. That bitch.

That was why Ayaan hadn't gone over there before now. She

knew, as God was her witness, that she would not be able to keep her temper down; and now the very thought of the heifer next door made her want to smack somebody.

How selfish can you be? She made the decision to not be a mother. She gave up the right to be anywhere close to her daughter. Now it would be different if Kendall had been asking about her. Kendall doesn't care about her birth mother. Not in the real sense. How could she? She doesn't even know where babies come from. Kendall knows she was adopted. Sure. How could that damn Shelia even believe there was any way for this to turn out right? Ayaan decided to walk another block. She knew walking wouldn't help. So she did something that she hadn't done in months. She called her ex-husband.

"I talked to Shelia. I'm on my way over."

Shelia

2003

Well, at least Ayaan didn't cut her. She couldn't blame her for being angry. Shelia should have been the one to take the first step. She should have been the one to try to explain how she felt. Even now, she knew Ayaan didn't believe that she didn't mean any harm. Ayaan was right. Even if Shelia didn't mean any harm, that didn't mean the situation wouldn't blow up in her face.

Kendall would be the one to pay the price. What's worse? Knowing your mother gave you up or knowing she gave you up, moved in next door, and still didn't take you? Either way she was screwed. Or even worse, your biological mother sued the only mother you've ever known to get custody of you and shatter any semblance of security that you had. The risks were high.

Even so, if she was completely honest with herself, she knew she would absolutely have made the same decision again. Shelia hadn't tackled life head-on like this since college. Even then, she wasn't particularly good at it without Zel's guidance.

1994

Shelia had always been the cautious sort. In high school, she was always the wallflower. For the longest time, she thought that it was because she wasn't attractive. She was a nerd: National Honor Society, Spanish Honor Society; but truthfully, Mother didn't allow her to date. So even if she wanted to approach a guy, it wasn't as if he could call her or she could call him. Mother believed it was her duty to monitor Shelia's calls. It wasn't just monitor, as in how many calls are coming in. It was more like try to pick up the phone, without Shelia knowing, to listen to her conversations.

Her friends tried to help by fixing her up with their boyfriend's best friends and brothers. Often Shelia got stuck watching really bad television, as minute by excruciating minute passed by, until a friend freed her by saying she was ready to go, or the blessed clock struck closer to the time when their ride was supposed to pick them up at the library.

It wasn't that she didn't want to talk to guys. All of her secret hiding places at home were full of Harlequin Romance books about women who were shy, but the perfect man brought them out of their shell; or of confident women who could just walk up to a man and get his attention—cocky, self-possessed women, who always knew where they were going and what they were doing.

Shelia would have loved to be one of them, but she didn't know how. On her sixteenth birthday, one of the longtime friends decided that she needed to have a surprise birthday party—complete with boys. However, Shelia didn't have any boys to invite, so Kyla imported some of her man's friends. How she convinced Mother to do this was still beyond Shelia's comprehension.

It was a great party, even with Mother coming in and out every

35

few minutes just to make sure everything was "all right." Embarrassing, yes; but as long as it was "all right" (translated to mean no girls were kissing boys, sitting on boys' laps, or even engaging in long involved conversations with boys), Mother was content.

Mother even invited other neighborhood mothers to sit in the living room with her. Actually, the party probably had more chaperones than all the homecoming festivities combined. The shocking part was that one of the guys in her gym class came. Danny was so cute.

Shelia had a secret crush on him the whole year. It must have been the green eyes that did Shelia in. He was nice and spoke to her. So the fact that he was at her Sweet Sixteen gave Shelia's heart a little cheer of hope, but that was stifled when Shelia learned he was at her party to talk with one of her friends who had recently broken up with her boyfriend.

For most girls, it would be no big deal. Most of the girls at the party would have gone on to the next man, but for Shelia, it was different. She was on the sidelines of her own birthday party. That was the year Shelia banned all mass birthday celebrations. Who wants to feel like an extra wheel at her own birthday party?

1997

In college, it was harder to sit on the sidelines when she kept getting swept up in "tropical storm Zel." She was one of those rare people who could read a chapter in a book once and retain all the information. It was disgusting. Zel was pulling straight B's in her classes. She would have probably done better, if it wasn't for the fact that attendance played a role in grades for most classes.

She'd come strolling in from a date or a party—often the morning after—and happily relate her escapades to Shelia.

But while Shelia felt honor-bound to join the campus NAACP, it was more to get Mother off of her back than any drive to effect change. She did meet some very nice people, but they didn't have the sparkle in their eyes that Zel had. They didn't carry the zest for life that Zel possessed. They didn't come to meetings with highly entertaining stories like Zel.

So, second quarter she asked Zel, "Would you mind if I went with you tonight?" Poor Zel, who wasn't shocked at anything, blinked twice, closed her eyes, opened them, and blinked again. "You do realize this party isn't at the library, right?"

"Of course, I know that."

"No books—music, dancing and men."

"I know. OK. I just need to get out for a while."

"Hallelujah and thank you, God!"

Shelia just gave Zel a look. There were some things she didn't understand. Zel's life wasn't like Shelia's. Zel's mother was phenomenal. A bit absent at times, but Mama T, as everyone called her, was great. She always sent Zel the best clothes. Their dorm room was littered with fifty-thousand storage devices. Dorm rooms really weren't made for clothes horses. Zel even went as far as storing some of her clothes in Shelia's closet. Most of Shelia's clothes were knit, took up little room, and didn't make that much of a difference.

"So let's see. First, we need to do something about your clothing."

"I was just going to wear a pair of black pants and a top—all purpose."

"The only purpose to that would be to fade into the background, and you've been there all semester. If you're coming out with me, you're coming out with a splash."

Splash was putting it mildly. Zel usually characterized party clothes in four ways—sexy, sassy, slutty good, and slutty bad. Sexy was a bit more mysterious and intriguing. Sassy drew attention, but with more of a fun personality to it. Slutty good was overtly displaying skin. Slutty bad—well, that was displaying so much skin that you might as well walk past the party and work the first corner you came to; or displaying skin that you had no business displaying because of your size or lack thereof.

Despite Zel's bid for sexy or slutty good, Shelia came out with a sassy outfit. She ended up in her average basic black slacks, but still felt a little exposed in the shiny red wrap-around top. It didn't help that Zel wouldn't let her pin the top so that the "V' wasn't as deep. Mother always described red as a color for the slutty bad. She did manage to convince Zel that there was no way on God's green earth that she would wear the matching red pants. OK. It was more that, even though they had the same basic body shape, Shelia's five-feet-four frame was a bit too short for the red pants to look right.

She also had a sleek new hairdo and a different name, Lia—a bit more exotic and a bit less average.

Lia felt the bass pounding before she even walked through the door of the Billiards Center—a prestigious name for the pool hall. Of course, there were also video games and bowling lanes. Lia actually referred to it as a broken down Dave and Buster's. She'd never been to the center before at night. She was a horrible pool player and an even worse bowler. And, as a trifecta, the only video games she was even remotely good at were Ms. Pac Mac and Tetris. Those games had disappeared long ago. So the billiards center was a waste of her time.

The Q Dogs of Omega Psi Phi had rented the back of the building for the party, but the front would still be used for pool and bowling until midnight.

Lia tugged at the bottom of her top, which won her a steely-eyed look from Zel; she'd told her that she looked phenomenal. There weren't many people at the party yet. Actually, they had passed a good-sized crowd in the gaming area. Zel was convinced that the crowd would be in later. This was prime time according to Zel. They could dance without having to worry about bumping into anyone.

Later they'd have to do the "I-know-it's-crowded-but-I-need-room elbow-throwing" dance—just a little jig that ensured that their personal space was respected. Zel said, "A well-placed elbow will get just about anyone to shift over. And whom can they blame? You were on the dance floor first." Since Zel rarely left the dance floor. She considered partying her aerobic workout and took it very seriously.

The combination of booming bass and familiar lyrics, "Nothing but House … music … all night long," with strobe lights, disco balls and a nearly empty dance floor were all Zel needed. With a whoop, she let the music pull her to the dance floor, as it pushed Lia directly to a nice little corner that managed to have an empty chair.

She could relax and still keep an eye on the comings and goings. She tried to inconspicuously pull the V-neck of her top closed a bit. The top just puckered giving a full view of her bra to anyone close enough to take a gander. *Can't win for losing.*

While she was preoccupied with that, Zel made her way over to her shadowy corner and pulled Lia onto the dance floor. Even though Lia rarely went to parties, she loved, loved, loved to dance. She could pick up dances in a drum beat and knew how to use the rhythm to her advantage. Of course, she had to stick with the "I'm not really dancing with anyone" dance. That dance required her to look at the floor or ceiling or at times close her eyes and pretend that the music was taking her over. Basically, she had to pretend that she didn't mind that she and Zel were on a practically empty dance floor and people were staring at them.

While Shelia's moves were cool and smooth, Zel's were bold and brassy. Zel even danced with attitude. She'd pick someone in the crowd, and it was almost like she was dancing with him. Zel liked to call it picking the litter. She'd make eye contact and go to work gyrating her hips, like all she was missing was a pole and some singles. It was sort of like being an artisan. And she always got her man—unless that man was there with someone else. Then, of course, there was always tomorrow.

By midnight, the party was kicking. The DJ was hitting and the crowd had started moving in from the gaming room. By midnight, Lia had begun dancing with guys … attractive guys. They were always friends of the guys that were drawn to Zel, but at least she wasn't on the dance floor alone. Zel's shine was giving her a bit as well. She wished she could be as free as Zel, but she had to think things through almost three times before making one move. But Zel, Zel was different. She was all in, 24/7.

By 12:30 a.m., Lia was bone tired and ready to go home. *How many hands did these guys have anyway*? They'd dance over all nice and average with two arms and two hands. Then when no one was looking, they'd grow a couple more. She'd swear under oath that these guys were at least a quarter octopus or something.

The more hands Lia moved from various parts of her body, the more hands there seemed to be. She'd move the one from her leg, another one from her butt, one from her arm, and another one from her back—not to mention the one holding her hand trying to pull her closer so he could grind on her.

Not only was she a bit disheveled because of the hands she had to constantly remove, but she was also a bit upset because these guys apparently didn't know how much they sweated when they danced. And not perspired and definitely not glistened, but Niagara Falls, River Nile, miles of sweat. Who wanted to be that close to a sweaty man?

Lia gave Zel that Universal "goin' to the bathroom" signal and made her way out the back door. Air. Blessed air. She meandered over to the line at the bathroom. She didn't mind waiting. This was much better than the sweatbox she just left.

She leaned her tired bones against the tile wall and immediately heard Mother's voice in her head. "Don't touch anything in a public restroom. Half the people don't wash their hands. So you don't know what kind of diseases they're spreading." Even from two hours away, her lectures stayed with Shelia, who straightened and waited her turn with proper Cordell posture.

After taking care of that business, she started to walk around to the front of the building to go back in the party, and suffer through a couple more hours of groping. She promised Zel that she'd stay until at least 3:00 a.m. before running back to the safety of her room. She had a project to work on at the library tomorrow, so she wanted to get at least a halfway decent night/morning of sleep. The pool area had muted lighting indicating that it was shut down for the night.

However, in the bowling area, there was a cute guy leaning against the wall. He stood way taller than six feet, with chocolate brown skin, sleepy eyes, closely faded black hair, and a divinely shaped pair of lips that had a bit of weight to them. Not enough to overpower his face, but enough to make you wonder. He had a Larenz Tate look about him—a sort of approachable attractiveness. He was holding court with his friend. Shelia figured that's what caught her attention. There was nothing that she secretly worshipped more than a confident man.

As she gave him what she thought was a discreet once-over, she noticed he was standing by the door in his sweat socks. He really didn't look like the Birkenstock, back-to-nature, or the sixties type. Actually, he looked well put together. He was wearing a cream knit top with his blue jeans, but he was in a public area hanging out in his sweat socks.

Looking up, Lia caught his eye. He must have seen her perplexed look, which of course was accompanied by a mild blush when their eyes met. Usually, when she made eye contact with a guy, she was quick to lower her head and scurry to her designated location, but something about this guy kept her eyes locked into his.

Then, he smiled. The blood stopped rushing to her face— merely because her heart stopped pumping. He had the most beautiful and inviting smile she had ever seen on a man. She just stopped walking and stared, mesmerized.

His smile changed to a cocky, sexy little smirk, and he pointed to the bowling area. Shelia noticed some guy laying his head on the scorer's table. He looked as if he had fallen asleep or passed out, but directly beneath his mouth, on the floor, were a pair of shoes covered in a vile-looking mixture that could only be produced from partial food digestion and too much alcohol.

Since the drunk guy was wearing his own shoes, Shelia quickly figured out what happened and let out a small giggle and gave "Shoeless Joe" an open, unfettered smile.

It was he who looked shocked for a minute.

Shelia immediately closed her mouth and headed back to the party.

The next day at noon, Shelia dragged herself out of bed. *My gosh. How did people do it?* She couldn't imagine going through this every weekend. She knew of others who managed a full course load and partied every weekend. Shelia couldn't imagine doing this more than once a month.

Even then, she had to maneuver. Mother knew her schedule and any deviation required an explanation. When Mother called at 9:00 a.m., Shelia said she wasn't feeling well and told her that she'd call her back later. Of course, this led to the third degree. Mother was sure that Shelia had imbibed in some alcoholic substance and gave her another unnecessary lecture about how hard she worked to get her where she was. It took half an hour to get Mother off the phone. Five minutes after that, Shelia was out like a light.

She looked in the mirror. Partying was hard work, especially for a girl who had made a habit of being in bed by 11:00 p.m. Her face showed it this morning. She had bags that were big enough for a two-week trip to Mexico living under her eyes.

Of course, she might have done a bit better if Zel had taken her home when the party at the center was over. They agreed on 3 a.m., but Zel had insisted on going to the after party. She was so excited. She saw it as a chance to meet more interesting men. Shelia saw it as a chance to fight off more sweaty guys and the lines—the lines were horrible.

Shelia had heard stories about piss-poor pick-up lines. She had even been on the receiving end of some pretty poor attempts, but come on. "Baby, I know your feet are tired, because you've been running through my mind all day." "You look so good, I just want to sop you up with a biscuit." And the most disturbing of them all from the Omega Psi Phi man (or better yet, Q Dog,) who simply asked to lick her. *Who responded to those lines, anyway? What would they say?*

"Oh yes, please go get a can of Hungry Jack biscuits and I'll meet you right here in twenty minutes." Or maybe, "I'm so excited to have the opportunity to be licked by someone who distinctly looks like a bulldog. Please proceed."

These are intelligent college students. They could probably solve complex physics equations, but couldn't come up with something besides a rundown of the characteristics that went with her Zodiac sign, "You a Libra girl. You know what that means. You're a freak"— like he would ever get a chance to know.

After a while, Zel got preoccupied with the guys, as she was prone to do. Thankfully, Shelia was able to retire to a corner. Only problem was she had gotten so sleepy just hanging out there that she began to nod off. As a safety precaution, she wound the strap of her purse around her wrist and hunkered down to wait until Zel was ready to leave.

She was in good company. There were some drunken people sawing logs in other corners. It was better they slept it off instead of spewing it up. This led Shelia's thoughts back to Shoeless Joe at the Billiards Center. She dozed with a smile on her lips.

Now it was noon on Sunday, she was bone tired and had to spend at least three hours in the library finishing her project. Oh, the humanity. Zel had disappeared after she dropped Lia off. She tried to convince her body to hurry. They stopped serving brunch in the cafeteria at 1 p.m., and Shelia hated missing meals that she already paid for.

She grabbed her shower bucket and worked her way to the community shower. Barely nodding to her floor mates, she wandered into the stall and tried to convince herself that she really was awake and her mind really was functioning. She started thinking how the Herbal Essences commercial lied blatantly. She sniffed at the body wash as if there was dope on the other end, but she didn't get that immediate regeneration that they displayed in the commercial. She ought to write a very stern letter to those Herbal Essence people because she got absolutely nothing from the experience.

She got dressed in jogging pants, pulled her hair back into a ponytail, and walked down to breakfast. She wished Zel had made it back before she went to the cafeteria. Shelia saw a couple of people from her floor, but no one she really felt comfortable eating with. Shelia found a seat close to a window and sat down. Had her mind been functioning properly, she would have thought to bring a book with her. When she didn't have anything to read, she took up her next favorite pastime.

She created stories in her head. Sometimes she was someone famous. This time she was an above-average-looking college student who loved to wear bright colors and take a firm hold on life. She imagined what would have happened if she had gone up and talked to Shoeless Joe. He would have looked at her and given her another one of those "Oh so sexy" smiles. She would have lightly touched his chest. "I think you're missing something."

"I know, my shoes are over there."

"Umm, I was thinking more like my number." She'd gently folded it and put it in his pocket. "Now don't let that become a decoration. I expect you to use it." Shelia always came up with the best lines when she was by herself.

She finished her greasy omelet and immediately trekked across the quad to the library. She collected the books she needed and put her feet up on the chair across from her, slouched down until her head was supported by the back of the chair, and prepared to read. After about a half an hour, she realized she wasn't going to make it without caffeine. She unwrapped the chocolate bar she smuggled in and took a quick break.

As her eyes became heavier, she figured resting them for a minute wouldn't hurt.

"You mean you didn't get enough sleep at the Q set."

Shelia jerked her eyes open in shock.

Standing before her was the shoeless guy from the center. He was, of course, looking well put together. *How could someone have partied as long as he must have the night before and still wake up presentable?* He was wearing jeans, gym shoes, and a cotton oxford—the kind of shirt that one has to iron. It was almost too much. He wasn't carrying bags under his eyes; he had partied the night before and was still walking around in clothes that had been ironed. Maybe he had a maid. And the voice. Not a scratchy rode-hard and put-away-wet note about. Baby had Boys II Men, Michael McCary bass.

Shelia hadn't had enough sleep for her normal conversation or even her I'm-not-interested-in-any-male conversation. She couldn't mentally figure out something flirty and appropriate to say to a cute guy who found her snoozing at the library in clothes befitting a vagabond. She'd steal one of Zel's lines if her brain would ever function fast enough to remember them; but it didn't, so she was on her own.

The minute Shelia opened her mouth, a huge yawn escaped. "I didn't see you at the after-set."

"You were busy sawing logs."

Embarrassed, Shelia looked down. "You know, I should probably get a Coke or something. I'm never going to make it through this studying without some caffeine."

"Here take mine."

"Sorry. Not allowed to take candy from strangers. Even if it comes in a perfectly innocent Coke can."

"You look like you could use a nap."

Shelia gave him a look which signified that it didn't take a rocket scientist to figure that out. "I was taking one before I got interrupted."

With that he smiled, the same brilliant smile that stopped her heart at the center and now took her tongue at the library. "Since you won't take my Coke, would you mind taking a phone number from a stranger?"

Shelia was stunned. "Hmm. Well." *Zel, Zel, what would Zel do? Think, think.* "Actually, I would mind, but I can go out on a limb and give you mine."

He took her number and said, "I'll talk to you later. By the way, you have a little something in your front teeth."

The red began to creep up her neck to her face. She took a mirror out of her bag and opened it. A little piece of peanut was nestled between her two front teeth. Great. "Umm, thanks for pointing that out. Well, umm, I guess I'll talk to you later?"

"Definitely."

As the guy now known as Rick walked away, Shelia ran through her mind all the things she could have said, but didn't. She could have asked if he got his shoes back. Maybe made a joke about wearing the bowling shoes home. She could have even inquired about the drunken friend. Nothing. She missed a prime opportunity, but someone had asked for her number. Shelia looked down at her book and smiled. She then felt a tickle on her neck. Looking up, she realized Rick was watching her from his seat across the room. Now, she wouldn't be able to stop smiling even if she wanted to.

That was the beginning of Shelia and Rick.

AYAAN

2003

Goodness knows that at some point in her life she was going to have to stop running to Kenneth. She had managed the financial part, but the emotional part was still a bit tricky. For the longest time, he was her very best friend. Even now, he was the only person who would understand what was happening. Her parents had died in a car crash when she was a senior in college. She was an only child. So she didn't have any family to get indignant. She had Kenneth.

One of these days, he was going to find someone who wouldn't appreciate their relationship. They still talked a few times a week, but Ayaan had made a point of not seeing him. It brought back all the reasons they could be great together. However, she knew it would never work out, because there was one major reason why it never did work out.

Ayaan scurried back to her car and headed for Kenneth's office. Technically, it was still their office, since she retained the rights to half of the business in the divorce settlement. They just couldn't work together anymore. He hired a public relations practitioner. She kept the business partner paycheck. It worked out well for her in a lot of ways. The problem was she still missed him every day. Even now on the half-hour drive into the city, she remembered everything about their first date.

1995

It was that first kiss. If she hadn't kissed him, it could have been so different. However, she did. She reached for the stars, and for a while she was flying high.

When they were just friends and business partners, Ayaan dressed for herself or the event. However, their first date was different. They'd known each other for years. They knew practically everything about each other. Yet, she stood in front of her closet in her lakefront loft and debated about what to wear. She had thought about it all day and still hadn't figured it out.

She wanted to look special, but not like she was "trying" too hard. Plus, she didn't want to wear something he had seen before. She probably should have gone shopping, but that would have defeated the purpose of not trying too hard. So she stood staring into her closet. She went from hanger to hanger. She only wore dresses when the occasion called for it. So for her to put on a dress now would have been a bit conspicuous. She usually wore jeans and dressed them up or down depending on the occasion. A blazer could work wonders. No one wore a blazer on a date. Did they?

Ayaan moved another hanger down on the rack. OK, what were her best assets? Thanks to a great genetic match, she looked good in whatever she wore. She got the ass from her mother's side and the boobs from her father's. Ayaan didn't have to impress Kenneth with her mind. He had known about that for years. However, this was a man that was used to dating twenty-year-old women. He always skewed younger—and then wondered why it never worked out.

It didn't take a degree in psychology to figure that out. Ayaan had met some of the women he had dated. They were all cute and fun. They all had a black Barbie doll complex. They had different creative occupations—models, actresses, musicians—but as females, they were carbon copies of each other. The models cared more about what they looked like, what they wore, where they were seen than, they did for their craft. The others were often more dedicated to him than their craft.

Not only was she competing with younger women, she was competing with younger women that doted on Kenneth. They cooked him meals, cleaned his house and took care of him. One of them even did his laundry. What was that?

Ayaan flopped down on the bed. Why did she kiss him? What was she really offering? She didn't mind doing laundry. She sort of had to, if she wanted clean clothes without the hassle and expense of taking everything to a professional laundry or dry cleaners. She cooked because, in addition to getting her boobs from her father's side of the family, she also got their love of food.

However, she had always been more of the business than domestic type. Given the option, everything business won over everything domestic.

Get yourself together, Ayaan. She had gone out with Kenneth plenty as business associates, but this was the first time they dated. Goodness knows, she never cooked him a meal. She had fixed salads, but that was the extent of his knowledge of her culinary skills.

Ayaan went back to her closet, determined to find something to wear. She raked through the hangers, dismissing one outfit after another. Then she found it. Wow. She had bought it years ago when she had vacationed in Montreal. It was a dusty rose summer dress with spaghetti straps and showed off all of her assets. She had been waiting to wear it, but it always seemed it was either too dressy or not dressy enough.

One good push-up bra to get the boobs to their twenty-year-old perkiness, and she'd be set to go. She didn't care if Kenneth thought she was trying too hard. She didn't care if he thought it was too dressy. Hopefully, after all this time, he wasn't planning on taking her to Burger King.

She put on the dress, found gray heels in her closet, and grabbed a small evening purse. She always kept her hair in perfect condition with weekly visits to her stylist. She looked in the mirror. She cleaned up pretty well. If she was trying too hard, was that really a bad thing? If anyone was worth the effort, it was Kenneth.

Ayaan looked at her watch, walked into the kitchen, and started pacing. She opened the refrigerator. However, if she ate something now, she ran the risk of spilling it on the dress or having food stuck in her teeth. So she went in the living room and gingerly sat on her couch, making sure she smoothed her dress.

She liked it a whole lot more when she and Kenneth were just friends. Then, she would have come to the door with food in hand and just waved him in. It was amazing how things shifted with one kiss. She laid her head on the back of the couch and inspected the ceiling. She looked at her watch again. He was late. He was never late. That was usually her role, because she tried to pack so much into a day that when evening rolled around she was always behind.

As she waited, she started to get annoyed. He could be on time for all the Barbie dolls, but he was late for her. This was a bad way to start anything.

Just as she contemplated the demise of a relationship that had yet to begin, she heard a knock on the door. There stood Kenneth adjusting his tie. Ayaan looked at him skeptically. Since she was used to telling him everything that came in her head, nothing could have prevented her from saying, "I didn't think you owned a suit. I've seen jeans and tuxes, but nothing in between."

Kenneth looked a bit uncomfortable. "Well, we've never been on a date before so … I could say that it was in the back of my closet, but the truth is it's new. Are you happy? I went shopping for you. You can't even start with 'Hi' or 'You look nice.' No, you have to start with the fact that I'm wearing a suit."

"Well," Ayaan said with a smirk, "it does look nice."

"Whatever. Might I add that I have never seen that particular dress. I thought you only wore dresses under protest."

"Well, I … at least I didn't go shopping. This was in the back of my closet."

Kenneth gave her that smile that pulled in those models, actresses, and musicians, and promised all kinds of bad intentions. "Well, thank God you found the good sense to move it to the front. Turn around. I want to know if you're wearing a thong. It looks thong-worthy."

Ayaan hit Kenneth on the arm. "What difference does it make to you? I don't show thongs on the first date."

"That doesn't really apply to me, because I've known you for years. I'm not some stranger off the street corner." He leaned in. "I'm your friend." He gently stroked her arm. "You know me."

For a quick second, Ayaan considered leaning into him for another kiss. If she had, she doubted they would have made it to the restaurant.

"Come on, Sweets. Come to daddy."

That's the benefit of, and trouble with, knowing someone that well. "For the record, I'm going to need you to come up with a new nickname for me." She grabbed her purse from the small table, eased out of the door, and closed it. "Sweets is what you use for the others. I'm not them."

Kenneth looked her in the eye and smiled. It wasn't a seductive smile. It was a genuinely happy smile. "No, you're not."

Under his breath, he mumbled something. Ayaan swore it was something like, "I've been waiting forever for you." She'd bet on it, but it couldn't be. Could it?

"Wait, what was that?"

He just smiled again and held out his elbow. "So tell. How long are you going to be able to stand those heels before you will absolutely have to sit down?"

Ayaan took his arm. "I could probably do about a couple of hours. These are more comfortable than most."

"Dancing?"

Ayaan contemplated and wiggled her toes in her shoes. "Yeah, I could do some dancing."

"Good." Kenneth looked her straight in the eye, and Ayaan saw a light there. He used his other hand to secure her hand in the curve of his arm. "I think this is going to be a late night. I feel like showing you off."

Ayaan never again questioned whether he wanted one of his models/actresses/musicians. His eyes told her he wanted her.

2003

Memories were a bitch. Now, his eyes said, "I'm listening intently to what you have to say." That was a big difference from what they once said.

As Ayaan was racing to Kenneth's office, she passed the John Hancock Center where they had their first date on the ninety-fifth floor in the Signature Room. She sighed. As her mother told her, all good things must come to an end—and that's exactly what happened to their intimate relationship. Their friendship, though, had survived.

She headed west on Fullerton until she made it to their office in Lincoln Park. She walked in and smiled at his staff, which consisted of a whopping three people. Most of their work was outsourced. However, they kept an administrative assistant, a public relations practioner, and a project manager on staff at the office. Everyone looked up to wave. The smiles turned to looks of concern when she gave a generic wave and headed straight for Kenneth's office.

She flopped down in a chair in front of his desk.

He got up and closed the door.

She pouted.

He looked amused.

It pissed her off more. "You don't understand. She moved in next door."

"She moved in next door last month. She hasn't done anything to you since. Matter of fact, wasn't it Kendall who invited her to her birthday party? Kendall reached out to her."

"She moved next door."

"OK. I'll give you that, but it was an open adoption. There were no secrets. Everything was out in the open. You said at the time that you wouldn't mind if Shelia was in Kendall's life. Remember?"

"Every once in a while, I'm going to need you to forget one thing I've said over the years. Damn. You're like a recorder. You're worse than Kendall." Ayaan leaned over and put her head in her hands. "What am I supposed to tell Kendall? I can't tell her, 'Surprise, here's your birth mother.'"

"Why is this so surprising to you?"

"She was in Paris. Paris, France. I didn't think she was going to move back. I definitely didn't think she was going to move in next door. I had sort of hoped she would have gotten stuck at the top of the Eiffel Tower."

"What the hell? Now she's Rapunzel—stuck in a tower until someone gets her out?"

"Not exactly."

"You do realize that even Rapunzel escaped?"

"That's why I didn't think of her as Rapunzel."

"That doesn't make sense. You sent her mail every year."

"I didn't say it made sense. That's just how I thought of her. The longer she stayed away from us, the more I wanted to believe that she would never return. Kendall and I have built a life together. We're good. I don't want it to change."

Kenneth came around the desk and knelt in front of Ayaan. "She knows you're her mother. She knows you. Kendall is your daughter. She tilts her head the way you do when she's making a decision. She throws her head back when she laughs, like you do. She even does a happy dance when someone puts food in front of her, like you do. She's your daughter." Kenneth tucked a strand of hair in back of her ear. "Life changes—you know that better than anyone. Yet nothing has stopped you. Figure out how to deal with this. You know you can."

Ayaan went back to pouting. "I don't want to."

"You could go to a psychiatrist. That might help you figure out what to do."

"Maybe."

"I never understood why you agreed to an open adoption, anyway. You are pretty much an all-or-nothing type of woman."

"I would have agreed to anything. Even today, with Shelia next door slowly driving me crazy, I wouldn't change anything. Wait. I might go back and put some moving provisions in the adoption agreement; other than that, I don't have much to complain about."

Kenneth got up and went back behind his desk. "I still know a few people in the hood. I can get Shelia handled for you. Nice and quiet like."

Ayaan laughed. "You've been threatening to have people dealt with 'nice and quiet like' for years. How come I've never met these 'people' you always refer to?"

"Then you'd be a witness. I'm protecting both of us."

Ayaan picked up a paper clip from his desk and threw it at him. She slouched deeper into her seat, closed her eyes, and put her head against the back. "I guess the honeymoon is over. I'll think about what you said about a shrink. That might be the best route."

"Of course I'm right, Sweets."

Ayaan cracked one eye open. "OK now. I told you about that."

Kenneth laughed, and gave her that slightly naughty smile. "I must have forgotten. I meant to say, of course I'm right, Luv."

Ayaan let the endearment smooth over her emotions like aloe vera on a burn—soothing with a twinge of lingering pain.

"Now, tell me how you're growing our business. Momma needs a new pair of shoes."

"Right, then momma should get her happy ass in the office and start working. You see the books every quarter. We're growing fine." Even with that, Kenneth brought her up to date on the latest plans for expansion into other major cities.

When she left, she felt much better. Kenneth had that effect. He didn't coddle her; he told her the truth. There were times, though, that she could still see something of their old relationship in his eyes. That's why she didn't see him more often than she did.

One day he was going to find someone who fit him like a glove. Maybe then she would be free to find someone to fit her. Right now, she knew in the back of her mind that she was still holding his spot in her life. She knew in her heart it was only a matter of time before she stuck her tongue down his throat again, whether it made good sense or not.

Shelia

2003

Ayaan's visit was still on the top of Shelia's mind. She used to be a better planner. In school, she juggled her schedule like a pro. She had figured out how to party, date, and get grades good enough to keep Mother off that highway. There was a time when everything was better.

1997

She let her mind drift back to those days. Shelia stood in front of her mirror, while Zel tried to help her with her outfit, but Zel made her nervous.

"You have to show a little more skin. Get him interested."

"He is interested, and I haven't shown him a lot of skin."

"Studying and class are different from dates. For dates, you need to go way out. Give him a little more Lia and a little less Shelia."

"What you mean is you want me to be a little more Sybil? Split personalities?"

"No, see. It's the difference between someone saying, 'Could you move it along' in a New York accent and then in French. The message is the same, but the delivery makes the difference."

Shelia looked Zel up and down.

Zel had this innocent air that immediately signaled something was amiss.

"So you managed to meet the French student living in the International dorm, hmm?"

"What makes you say that?"

"You met the French guy that you said made your panties wet at the poetry reading."

"Shelia, come on. How would I meet him?"

"You met him, and you did him—and you kept it from me."

Shelia was having fun. It was rare that Zel didn't flaunt her relationships. Hell, she loved floating through the door with a satisfied gate, plopping down on the bottom bunk where Shelia slept, and giving her one detail too many. "What gives, Zel?"

"We haven't slept together. Thank you very much, but we have met; and baby, let me tell you—he might have actually told me to go to hell, but I didn't understand and didn't care. Brother is fine! Now let's get you out of my video and back into yours. We could always try a bustier with a jacket."

Zel was good at changing the subject. She knew Shelia would balk at the bustier. After an hour of "helping," Shelia kicked Zel out. "This is a date, not a funeral," Zel said before departing in a huff.

She had a half hour before Rick showed up, and she was barely dressed. The one piece of Zel's advice that she did follow, was not to wear all black.

French guy, eh? Shelia was definitely going to have to find out more about that one. She began raiding the clothes in her closet.

Since half of them were Zel's, there was quite a bit of color to choose from. Shelia compromised and chose a white and black silk blouse to go with her black slacks. Shelia was very afraid that if she chose an actual color that she'd sweat through it halfway through the night. Plus, they were going to IHOP. One doesn't dress up for IHOP.

Shelia got a phone call from downstairs. "Hey lady, are you ready?"

"Sure, here I come."

Shelia waited a few minutes to get her nerves under control. Thank goodness for the all-girl dorm. She smiled a bit. She once asked Zel, who loved men, why she was in an all-girl dorm.

Zel looked at her like she had temporarily taken leave of her senses.

"Have you seen the co-ed dorms?'

Shelia shook her head.

"They're just nasty. Beer bottles and pizza boxes galore and, if you hadn't noticed, I don't like men invading my space. I prefer to invade theirs."

Her memory of Zel helped lighten her anxiety. She was reaching for the door when the phone rang. Instinct had her answering before thinking. It was Mother.

"You remember my friend Darlene from work? She's the Director of Human Resources. Her son just finished graduate work in molecular biology."

"Mother, you do realize that science is more prestige than cash."

"Actually, he's going to do patent or trademark work or something like that. Darlene explained that he'd be really successful and has quite a bit of cash. How about I set up a date for the two of you the next time you come in town?"

"Mother, you do whatever you feel is best. I was actually heading to the study lounge. Big test in 'poly sci' coming up. Can we continue this conversation later?"

"Sure. Go study. Did you eat?"

"I ate a little something. I wasn't very hungry."

"You have to eat. Not enough to gain that freshman fifteen they're always talking about, but enough to maintain your current figure. Can't have you looking like you have an eating disorder, can we?"

"Oh, uh-huh. Well thanks for calling, Mother. I'll give you a call tomorrow."

Eating disorder? What kind of mother describes her daughter's looks that way? Didn't any of Mother's friends have girls? Or did Mother disown them the minute she found out they didn't have marriage-aged boys for her daughter to play house with?

Mother had ruined Shelia's mood on two counts. One, there was this cute guy downstairs waiting for her, and she had kept him waiting because Mother's timing, as usual, was impeccable; and two, she was more than a bit irked that Mother was trying to fix her up with yet another guy.

But as Shelia pressed the elevator button to go downstairs, she realized that Mother was two hours away. Shelia didn't have to answer the phone or call her back. Shelia was indeed free. She'd just have to maintain enough contact so Mother wouldn't drive up there and sit in the lobby until Shelia showed up.

As the elevator descended, her mood lifted. She was building a life, a life without Mother, a life of her choosing. She'd have to write that down somewhere because she was sure to forget.

She was going on a date with a cute guy who chose her. Mother couldn't tell her what time to be home. Mother didn't have Rick's mother on the horn discussing how great it would be if "the kids" got together. Mother was home. Shelia was stepping out on her date with a new attitude.

Rick stood when Shelia entered the lobby. He was wearing jeans. The top was a short-sleeved, deep-gray silk number that draped over his frame as if it was custom-made for him. He looked delicious.

When Shelia passed through the double doors of IHOP, the only thing that kept her semi-stable was the fact that Rick's hand was lightly guiding the small of her back. Of course, that was probably what was also causing her to sweat under her jacket. Good wardrobe choice.

As the waitress guided them to their seats, she noticed Rick nod to a few people. However, he didn't stop or even slow down.

He sat down across from her and smiled. "Is that a new blouse? You've never worn that to class."

Shelia answered slowly, "No, it's my roommate's. How would you know what I wear to class?"

"Well you always sit up front. I prefer sitting in the back because, as you can probably tell, I'm usually running a few minutes late. Plus, you're always doing crazy stuff."

Shelia looked at him as if he had sprung two heads, "Crazy stuff? I don't do anything crazy."

"You know what you do."

Shelia frowned, wracking her brain about what he meant. Finally, she asked him, "What?"

"Like paying attention and answering questions. What's that all about?"

Shelia began to blush. As the silence stretched, the syrup container began rattling against the salt and pepper shaker. Shelia looked around to see who was in IHOP.

Rick looked, stared at condiments, and separated them. He noticed that the table was slightly jittery. When he looked under the table, he noticed it was Shelia's leg that had the table shaking and shimmying. "So are you nervous or bored?"

"Excuse me?"

"The way the table is shaking, I figure it has to be one or the other."

Shelia's mouth dropped open. She never met someone who was that upfront about what they were thinking. She didn't have any experience fielding questions with anything except honesty. She could only play the what-would-Zel-do game for so long."

"I guess maybe I'm a bit nervous. I'm not one for nervous chatter, so my leg just takes over."

Rick's eyes began to soften, and the cocky smirk began to light the corners of his lips. "So I make you nervous."

"No, you bore me. I'm nervous because I'm not sure how I'm going to get to the door fast enough."

Rick laughed out loud, causing patrons to stare and Shelia to squirm.

"Well, Lia. I could do a table dance. Would that interest you?"

"Umm. I don't have any quarters to put in your G-string."

"Quarters? Quarters? Baby, when I move, people throw tens. I could show you."

Shelia held up her hands and laughed. "I believe you. I believe you!"

The telltale color began to creep up her neck the minute he mentioned the table dance, and it didn't get any better when she mentioned G-strings.

Rick looked at her closely. "I've never seen anyone who blushes as easily as you do."

"I've never met anyone who thinks it's necessary to point out every fault a woman has. I guess we're even."

Shrugging, Rick asked, "Who's pointing out faults?"

"You criticize constantly."

"That, my dear, is conversation."

Shelia felt herself pouting, but she couldn't help it. "Try conversing positively."

"Fine. I like when you give me a little shit. Don't get me wrong, I think the sensitive shit is cute too. I think you're cute too."

Shelia was in no way prepared for him being attracted to her. Intellectually, she knew she was on a date. To hear that he thought she was cute, she was nervous enough. That information was already coursing through the mind with no place to land. So she ignored it. "I'm not sensitive."

Rick let out a slight guffaw. "Really? Then how come you take back or try to explain half the things that fall out of your mouth?"

"Just for clarification."

"You're afraid to say what you mean."

Narrowing her eyes, Shelia responded, "I think I'm going to get over that rather quickly."

The waitress showed up to take their order. Shelia ended up with a "Rooty Tooty Fresh n' Fruity," if for no other reason than the name. Rick ordered a Denver omelet.

After the food arrived, Rick pointed to Shelia's plates, "That's a lot of food. Are you sure you're going to be able to finish it?"

"It doesn't matter if I finish or not. You have the bill."

"What happened to going Dutch?"

Shelia pushed the first bite of pancake into her mouth. "Only works in Holland, babe."

"So I'm your babe now."

Instant blush. "Sorry. That position is not given. It's earned."

"Tell me, Lia. What are the prerequisites?"

"It starts with home training, and since we know that you failed that, you're pretty much a lost cause."

Rick laughed. "You, my dear, are quick with the tongue. I like that."

"I'm glad I have your approval," Shelia mumbled.

"Didn't at least one of your etiquette books talk about enunciation?"

"Go to hell." It was out of her mouth before Shelia could think. Shelia clamped her hand over her mouth and looked at Rick with absolute horror.

"So you do curse. That's nice to know. Now if one day you manage it without looking like you've accidentally stabbed your brother, it would be even better."

"I'm sorry. I didn't mean that."

"Please, Lia. Yes, you did. You don't have to apologize. I'm a big boy. If I couldn't handle it, I wouldn't be here. Hell, I want to handle it—it, you, the whole package."

Too much. If Shelia knew one thing for certain, she was in over her head. Zel could rock this date as easy as breathing. Shelia was too scared of fucking something up to even enjoy it. Shit. Now she was cursing in her head. That was a clear indication it was time to run for cover. She took a deep breath. "Rick, I'm not sure I want to go there with you. You're a nice guy, but I don't think anything else is feasible at this point in time."

Rick stared at her for a minute. "I know what I want and like. That hoity-toity attitude isn't turning me away. I like a woman I can spar with, talk to. This is going to happen. Fuck 'feasible.'"

Shelia lowered her head to concentrate on her meal. Fuck feasible. You couldn't argue with that logic.

When Shelia got home that evening, she was smiling that kind of wide smile that can't be stopped or hidden. Sometimes a person doesn't even know that he or she is doing it. Not that it matters, because realization just makes the person smile more. Shelia was nodding her head to an imaginary tune only to be greeted by Zel the minute she opened the door.

"About time!"

Shelia jumped with her hand on her chest. "Damn, Zel. You just took ten years off of my life."

"Yeah, whatever —details, I need details."

"Can't I just tell you tomorrow? I'm a bit tired." Shelia barely maintained a straight face.

Zel's eyes got so narrow; Shelia was amazed she could still see. Zel really wasn't used to hearing, "No." Zel gave her a hard eye. "Don't do that to me. I suggest you sit down and give me details. I don't have time for your games."

"Well, then. I went on a date. I had a good time, and now I'm going to bed."

Zel stared for a minute. "You're right. I see you're tired." Zel unfolded herself from the bed and leisurely meandered over to the desk. "I'll just call Rick and see what he thought."

Shelia's mouth dropped and her eyes popped wide open. "You wouldn't."

Zel picked up the phone. "That's why you shouldn't be so organized. See if you leave a number by the phone, then I have access to call." Zel stood with one hand on her hip and the other one swinging the phone cord to and fro. "Well, Lia?"

"Fine, I'll talk—but for the record, I do hate you."

"Get over it."

Shelia sat on her bed and smiled thinking back to her night and the little things. Like how he opened the door, and he walked on the outside beside the curb, and he didn't turn around and look at other people … okay … other women, and he'd look into her eyes and smile.

Zel sat hard on Shelia's bed and interrupted her reverie. "Will you please tell me what's putting that silly grin on your face or I will call Rick? I really can't stand this suspense."

"Well, he picked me up, took me to IHOP. We talked. We laughed. We had a good time."

"Those aren't details."

"I don't know. We talked about school and stuff."

Zel smiled, "Did you talk about Mother?"

"Not quite. He knows I have a mother. Does that count for anything?"

"No. But skip her."

"Well, I kinda like him. He's nice," Shelia said smiling again.

"Did you plan a second date? Did you get any lip action?"

"He said he'd call me tomorrow."

"Hmm."

"Is that bad? Is it a brush-off?"

"We'll see tomorrow. Lip action?"

"Maybe."

Zel shook her by the shoulders until Shelia cracked up laughing. She broke free, grabbed her shower bucket, and ran for the door.

Zel threw a pillow at her.

Shelia ducked, opened the door, turned, and smiled. "His lips were like butter. So soft, full, soft, smooth; I melted."

Zel looked at her quizzically.

"Why are you looking at me like that?"

"I don't think I've ever seen your eyes sparkle like that. They're really pretty."

Shelia scrunched up her nose. "Thanks." She headed down the hall to the bathroom.

Turns out, Shelia didn't have to wait for the next day for Rick's call.

When she got back to her room, Zel was in bed with a smug smile.

"So I talked to Rick."

"You didn't."

"But of course, I told you I would. He had some very interesting things to say about tonight."

Shelia's face fell and the sparkle left her eyes. She looked defeated. "Hmm."

Zel looked up, "What's wrong?"

"Why would you call him?" The zest had left Shelia's step. "Couldn't you just let it be? It's our relationship or dating or whatever it is. I just wanted it to be us, you know."

Zel hopped off her bed and walked over to Shelia's. "Baby, I didn't call him. I know you haven't progressed that far. Come on. You should know me better than that; but if you don't, know this: I'd never do anything to harm your relationship, and I do count it as a relationship, because if I harmed it then you may go back to being stuck hiding behind these dang-on books. I need a 'kickin' it' partner."

Shelia smiled and sniffed at the same time. "Sorry, I guess I'm so used to Mother being all up in the business."

"But don't get me wrong. Butter lips did call. I just told him you were indisposed at the moment. Call him back. Baby, I won't intrude on your relationship. I'm just so happy you're dipping your toe into life, there is no way I'm going to jeopardize it with my curiosity. However, so you know, this good will only last for three weeks, so get your secret on now, because later I'll be all up in the grill."

Shelia laughed out loud. "I'm sure you will." Shelia went to the desk to pick up the phone. "Are you going to listen to every word I say?"

"Hell, yeah! But I promise not to comment on a thing, at least not too loudly."

Zel went to her closet and unearthed her headphones. Definitely a difficult task, because they were buried under at least a dozen or so pairs of size eleven shoes still in their original boxes, more or less. Not to mention the other shoe boxes, which contained her little toys—condoms, cuffs, clit cream and condiments. Poor Shelia would probably faint dead away if she knew about those.

Zel looked at Shelia as she tried to have a semi-private conversation. She put on her headphones to make it a smidge easier. Oh, she could still hear every semi-delicious drop of conversation, but at least it would give Shelia the "I-want-this-relationship-to-be-about-us-roommate" illusion that she wasn't paying attention.

Shelia was so very ... virginal. If she had a little more confidence, she'd be really pretty. As it stood now, she came across as being so innocent—so pure and untouched.

AYAAN

2003

There is nothing better than love. Luther Vandross taught Ayaan that. For a while, she had believed in that promise with everything that she had. Between Luther, Disney, and Harlequin, she had no doubt she was going to meet the man of her dreams. He would sweep her off her feet, and she would live "happily ever after."

She waited for that. She waited for Kenneth. Now, truth be told, they had the normal issues that couples have. He left the toilet seat up. She never made the bed. He took the dishes out of the rack as soon as the dishwashing cycle was finished. She believed that filling and emptying the dishwasher as needed was sufficient. She firmly believed that cars were a man's responsibility—washing, oil changes, all of it—and firmly handed that over the Kenneth.

He was more a part of the women-can-do-anything than the man-can-do-anything camp. Ayaan believed that as well, but she was happy to hand over some of what she believed were the inconsequential reigns to Kenneth. He grumbled, but she didn't care as long as he continued to change her oil. So it wasn't perfect.

Even with Disney et al., Ayaan hadn't been looking for perfect. She was looking for honest and true. That was hard enough to get. She had enough failed relationships to know that honesty was as elusive as the Loch Ness Monster. People kept claiming sightings of open-and-honest relationships, but rarely had she any proof of one.

Ayaan had already been through the ringer with one relationship. She had met Vince in college. He was a Kappa through and through. The man was fine, and he knew it. A woman had to be confident to approach a man that could literally spend more time in the bathroom getting ready than she did. Ayaan wasn't half-stepping now. She had pulled better. Her first impression was that he was about one inch deep. What other impression could she get from a male that spent that much time ironing his clothes?

Vince had approached Ayaan at a mutual friend's house. She had heard rumors that he was a "hoe" of the first order—shallow and a hoe. He really thought his presence alone was enough to pick up women. It might have worked for him in the past; it wasn't enough to pick up Ayaan.

The first time he tried to holler at her, she turned him down. When he asked why, she told him flat out that he was a hoe. She didn't date hoes. It was a waste of time.

He continued to pursue.

Ayaan was into her studies and spent most weekends at the library. She would also spend time at poetry readings, dance performances, and with other artistic pursuits.

It started when he showed up at Ayaan's house uninvited. Well, not completely uninvited, but uninvited by Ayaan. He convinced her roommate to invite him over for dinner. Ayaan ate in her room.

When he showed up at the NAACP discussion of *The Bluest Eye*, he actually made some good points as they deconstructed the novel. Who knew there was a brain behind all that? So they talked. He gave her more than his normal pickup mantra, and she was intrigued. When she found out he could sing, too, she was hooked.

Ayaan always liked to believe she was the complete package. She was pretty, smart, creative, athletic. What man wouldn't want her? Vince. Vince didn't want her. Even though they went out for three years, she wasn't enough for him. Not really. He loved her in a way, but he really loved the conquest. The first year they were together was great—the next year, not so much. While she came up the front stairs of his off-campus apartment, there'd be someone sneaking out the back.

Ayaan wanted it to work. She excelled at so much that she didn't realize that she couldn't make a relationship succeed by the sheer force of will. The third year they were together, they decided to have an open relationship; so he wasn't technically cheating. As long as she came first, it was all good.

Of all the ideas she could have come up with to save the relationship, that one was the worst. She gave her boyfriend the option to sleep with other women. True, he was doing it already. However, she wasn't. So he was free to be the hoe of the world, sowing his royal oats; and she was being the open, liberated woman that she envisioned herself to be.

So what if he never took these other women out on dates? So what if he was as discreet as one could get on a college campus?

Then it got worse. She started competing with the tricks he was dating. She was pulling out all the stops in the bedroom. She had tools, outfits, props, "the whole nine." She was miserable, and Vince was in heaven. However, a college student rarely had a budget for food and clothing for school. There wasn't a budget for fishnets. Out came the credit card. Now she was broke and desperate. He was sleeping around and, as a reward, he had a girlfriend who was slowly elevating her game to porn star status.

It was not a good time in Ayaan's life. Finally, a friend sat her down and gave her a lecture that she would never forget. "Enough is enough. Damn. He can't be worth all of this maintenance. Trust me. There is better out there," Kadira said.

"Another one won't be Vince," Ayaan replied

"Thank God."

Ayaan paused. Kadira was right. She was tired, exhausted and ready to admit defeat. She had to know "when to hold 'em and when to fold 'em." Clearly, it was time to fold. She learned one valuable lesson from that debacle. Children without siblings never really learned to share their toys.

While Ayaan dated after college, she didn't come close to the love of her life. Often people asked her about her single status, but she didn't care. Single and celibate were two different things. She could enjoy the men she was with without the drama that came with it.

She always rationalized it by saying she could still be with Vince, but being single was definitely better than that madness. Being with Kenneth trumped both the Vince madness and being single.

1995

When Kenneth turned on the charm, it wasn't oily and slick, it was like a strong grip. He held her up. On their first anniversary, Kenneth asked her to meet him at his sister's Crystal's house. Ayaan didn't think two things about it. Ayaan was close to Kenneth's sister. Apparently, Kenneth's brother-in-law had gotten a huge bonus at work and surprised his wife with a square-cut, yellow diamond ring. Ayaan and Crystal must have spent fifteen minutes oohing and ahhing over the ring.

In the car, Ayaan immediately asked the first question that had come to her mind, "Do you think he's cheating?"

Kenneth paused, "Why can't he do something nice for my sister without having to cheat?"

Snorting, Ayaan replied, "This is the man that parked half a mile away to avoid paying for valet. He's that cheap. That ring didn't look cheap at all."

"Ayaan, I'm sure he's not cheating. He better not be. I have people that will take care of that."

Ayaan smiled and closed her eyes. "Ahh, the infamous people."

"You better believe," Kenneth confirmed.

"So where are we going? It better be somewhere good. I had to dig out my heels for this one."

"You are so spoiled. Can't I have one surprise?"

The evening started out alright. They ate. They went to All Jokes Aside and had a few laughs. It was their drive home that changed everything. At the time, Kenneth was living on South Shore Drive in an apartment overlooking Lake Michigan. They are driving down Lake Shore Drive when Kenneth pulled off to 35th Street.

"What's going on?"

"Let's sit on the lakefront for a while."

Everyone in Chicago knows the parks close at dark. Everyone also knows that no one really cares when the parks close. Even after dark, it's filled with cars, usually young people making out. The fact that she and Kenneth were a bit older didn't bother Ayaan very much. It was her anniversary. She was due for a little "wildin' out." When they parked, Kenneth got out of the car. He pulled out a blanket, two wine glasses, and a little cooler with champagne.

Ayaan was shocked. It was her trunk, after all. When did all that stuff magically appear? While she was enraptured by the ring, he'd been adding stuff to her trunk.

He grabbed her by the hand and pulled her away from the car a bit. He spread the blanket on the ground and popped the champagne. She lay down beside him and they began talking, drinking, and laughing. Sometimes they were silent, listening to the waves lap up against the barriers. They managed a good forty-five minutes before the police came to clear out the park, as they had to do multiple times a night. It was in those forty-five minutes that Ayaan knew that she wanted to spend the rest of her life loving her very best friend.

Zel

2003

Zel was killing time in Paris. She could have easily left earlier for the States, but she wasn't quite ready. Zel looked around her apartment. She had come up since the time that Shelia lived with her, but it wasn't like she was a straight "super model." Her money came from personal appearances, as much as from her modeling and designing.

She was a personality, as her manager described it. She didn't know when she became a personality. True, she didn't have a sensor on her tongue, but that could have gone two ways. She could have just as easily been blackballed. Her people called her refreshingly honest. It made Zel laugh out loud. Someone up there obviously liked her. If not, her career would have lasted as long as ... well, she used to say a white man's dick, but Etienne killed that analogy. Wow.

Zel loved her life but, she would be the first to admit, there was something missing. She thought, at one point, it was a child. However, she later narrowed it down to love—unconditional love. She could be loud, bawdy, or quiet; and he'd understand while loving her anyway. She wanted someone that she didn't have to explain everything to, someone who was smart enough and patient enough to *get* her.

Etienne described her as a handful once in a magazine. She was grateful. She had put that man through an emotional ringer. Rumor had it that he went straight from their breakup to the shrink's couch.

Sometimes she wanted to be bothered. Other times she just didn't. He was a sensitive artist type. They should have known better. Chemistry is a bitch. They should have waited before having sex. However, if they had gotten to know each other first, they would have never gotten to the fact that all white men have little penises is truly just a myth. Maybe it was American white men. Zel would have to add that to her list of experiments.

Zel walked over to the window, which looked out onto a shared garden. She lived on the first floor. At first that made her a little nervous, but she liked the ability to open her windows and enjoy what others in the building had to walk to. When she didn't want to be bothered, she simply closed her windows. She should probably move. Every year, it seemed she had the money to do it, but she didn't—laziness maybe. It could be the sense of the familiar. Plus, everyone around here knew her and so never really bothered her. She didn't need more space. She didn't need more amenities.

She used to say she'd move when she found a man worth moving for. Well, men worth cumming for and men worth going for are two distinct and often contradicting types. Zel smiled at her own play on words. She inhaled the scent from the garden.

So, Shelia was getting herself together. Zel figured that process could take forever. Shelia had been so messed-up from the beginning. Even in college, Zel had to look after her a bit. Shelia was a bit naïve, but, at least she knew it and did her best to stay in the background. When she started dating Rick, who was definitely not a background player, Zel had started out concerned. A lot of freshmen were getting caught up with players on campus.

1997

Zel had Rick checked out. He definitely dated; and from what she heard, he was definitely a crowd pleaser both on the court and in the bedroom. However, bed hoppin' wasn't his style. The only unsatisfied customers she found were the misguided hoochies that equated sex with a relationship. Hell, if you're going to give up the drawers just because the guy can dribble, and the only reason you know his last name is because it's stitched on the back of his jersey, you really can't expect a lifetime commitment.

Rick definitely wasn't a wallflower, but his rep was intact. Zel kept an eye on him just to make sure.

It wasn't hard to put out a few feelers; there were only about fifty halfway decent black males on the campus. Of course, there was also what Zel liked to call the "others," a very elite group of young black men who either couldn't get into or stay in Carlington University. They just went to the local community college and hung out on the campus quad, at the library and at parties.

Every once in a while Zel gave them a little holler just for fun. Zel understood the game. If you're looking for something deeper than a quick in and out, then you have to act like it. Zel definitely had a healthy respect for sex and worshipped at its altar whenever she felt the need. However, very few people would understand that she only had sex with two people since she arrived on campus. Those two she tried just out of curiosity. Her neighborhood wasn't teaming with a variety of cultures, and she wanted to see what they brought to the table. She still smiled at her memories of Jin, the Asian was a bad boy. Zel loved naughty.

Zel knew deep down she wanted that connection with that one person. There was a time she thought she was a free spirit. Losing her virginity, she felt was a rite of passage. She did it logically with a man that was twenty-five years old to her sixteen. She had heard boys her age didn't know what they were doing. She wasn't chancing it.

Even still, she did it too lightly, only to realize later the value of her body. That still weighed on her a bit. She still had sex. She wasn't crazy. Some orgasms are totally worth it. However, she didn't take sex lightly.

Thing was, she just loved to sleep next to someone. There was just something about waking up entangled in someone's arms and legs that just made her feel content. Sometimes the guys got a little too active, but Zel had been in this game long enough to pick up a few things.

Like last week, Steven had gotten a bit cocky. Green eyes on a black man will do that. Steven was so used to females swoonin' at his feet that he forgot a few basics. They were sitting in his car, kissing up a storm. Tongues were flying left and right, hands venturing up, down, and around. Poor confused Steven said, "Let's go back to your place."

Zel looked at him, shocked, "Babe, that won't work."

"Why not? I'm into you. You're into me. We can do this."

Zel looked so very amused. "Can we now?"

"Yeah, Boo. You'll be so sprung you'll never want to leave."

"Will I now?"

"Come on, Zel, you know the deal. Why're you trippin'?"

"Steven, babe, one, I never do anything at my place. Two, you have a woman at home. Remember her? The one I met last week. Three, I only wanted a taste, not the full meal."

"But, I know the taste gave you a craving for the good stuff."

"Love, I am the good stuff. And, basically, you're not worthy."

Thinking about it, Zel had to admit, she liked being a tease. She loved being sought after, loved getting propositioned; loved the attention she drew—probably because growing up dark-skinned hadn't been easy on her. When she was young, her "friends" used to call her skillet, tar baby, and anything else they could think of to make her feel like shit. Her height didn't help either.

One day after school, Mama T was supposed to pick up her friend Tonia, and Tonia's brother from school; but when Mama T pulled up, Tonia flat out refused to get in the car.

"I don't want to go with her. Nobody likes her."

The brother, who wanted a ride, tried to convince Tonia to get in the car.

"No. I don't want to. They may try to take us back to Africa where they came from."

Now Mama T is not a nice woman on a good day and when you insult her and her daughter, all hell is likely to break loose. "Girl, if you don't get your narrow ass in my car, I will light it up like the Fourth of July. The only reason I'm still taking you home is because I told your momma I would; but know this, this is the last time you will come anywhere near me and mine."

Tonia may have been rude, but she wasn't rude and crazy. She sat quietly in the back seat. When Mama T dropped them off, she went inside and told that girl's momma a thing or three. Their momma asked Mama T to provide another ride for the ingrate, but that's not how Mama T' rolls.'

Mama T had her own belief system. It wasn't really based on religion. It was totally based on her personality and what she felt was right and wrong. That left a lot of room for interpretation. Zel learned at an early age that she better have a logical reason for doing anything, and if Mama didn't agree, Zel better be able to convince her with logic to support it or it was "a wrap."

Mama T attributed it to the fact that she was a designer and an entrepreneur. She had to believe in what she was doing whole-heartedly, because she had to get other people energized about it as well. That often did not leave room for negotiation. So in this case, taking that little girl home was already against her belief system. To swallow her emotions and keep taking Tonia home was more than Mama T could bear.

Mama T once said, "I wake up every morning and look myself

in the mirror and smile, because I like me. If I'm doing some shit that I know is wrong, there is no smile. So when I'm making major decisions, I think of that mirror. If I know that I won't be able to look myself in the eye, I don't do it. I've left some money on the table doing that. No doubt. But fuck it. It's money. I'll take peace with myself over rich and famous any day."

She said the girl wasn't welcome, and that was the end. Actually she said, she didn't care if an unmarked passenger van, with a strange white man, with candy and pedophile tattooed on his forehead rolled up on the curb next to Tonia, she still wasn't letting that little hussy in her car. Zel was almost positive that was a joke. Then again, once you pissed off Mama T to that extreme, she was pretty much done with you.

Mama T spent almost the whole ride home mumbling about ungrateful children and how obviously some children don't know how to act in public and how she should have left the girl there.

She also had choice words for Zel. "If you ever let someone stand there and disrespect you like that, I will pull your pants down where you stand and beat that tail like it's never been beat before. Believe that. I'm not fighting your fights for you. I can't smack someone else's child to the floor, but that's where that little bitch belongs. You do it, or you'll know what it feels like to have it done to you."

That, Zel believed.

In high school, she hit her stride. It helped that Designs by Tyla took off like a rocket and Mama T started designing for Zel. Plus, since Zel was so tall, she also worked as a model in Mama T's shows. How many of her other friends could claim to be a professional model?

Zel learned how to walk, how to talk, and most importantly, how to entice. She learned it so well that she earned an "A" in history class without lifting a finger or a skirt. A few select tears, a few sob stories, and a semester of admiration for the man that he was, had the teacher eating out of her hand. Granted, she probably would have gotten a "B" with no trouble at all, but why settle?

That was high school. This is now. And now she had her eye on Jacques. How can you not love the name Jacques? The minute she'd seen Jacques, it was all over. He was probably the finest guy on campus. Not the cutest, but the best package. Not referring to his stroke stick. Zel hoped that package was a contender. He had this smile that made Zel's love juice come down—and the voice. Admittedly, part of it may be the accent. Zel was a sucker for a man with an accent, except British, which didn't do a thing for her; Australian, who; Italian, hmm; Spanish—well for Spanish, Zel could just purr. Sometimes she did.

France already gave her the French kiss, which she dedicated many hard hours to perfecting. So why not give her the man to use her skills on?

Zel had met Jacques halfway through first semester, at the library, of all places. Even though she might not attend classes as often as her professors would like, she kept up with her reading. To do that, she had to get away from the distractions of men. Meaning she pretty much had to hibernate in the back corner of the library.

That day she was supposed to be writing a paper on romance languages for her world history class; and there he was, also in the history section. She had peeped him out before at a poetry reading, but that had been from a distance. Up close, he wasn't bad—tight little peanut ass. Zel really couldn't tolerate men with too much junk in the trunk. That was just nasty.

She was trying to squeeze by him in the aisle. Then he spoke, "Pardonez moi." She had heard he was from France, but the reality was a thing of beauty.

Zel stopped right behind him forcing his nose to stay in the books. He shifted and turned back to see if she had stopped for a reason.

Zel looked him up and down—definitely worth the price of admission.

"Sorry, didn't mean to squeeze you."

"Oh, it's no problem at all."

"Are you from France?"

Jacques laughed. "Lucky guess."

Zel's bud was awakened by the drowning love juices, and it started throbbing. It knew what it wanted—and it wanted him. Zel rarely got a reaction like this from her body, so she needed to reward it by giving it exactly what it wanted.

"I'm Zel."

"Jacques."

"How long have you been in America?"

"Just since the beginning of semester."

"Welcome. Make sure you take advantage of everything this great country has to offer. Here's my number." She took his hand and began to write the appropriate digits.

"Well, Zel. You are forward."

"Forward works well for me. Horizontal works better."

"Hmm."

"Talk to you later?"

Jacques never called. One day. Two days. Three days. Never called. Not that Zel sat in her dorm room. That wasn't her style, but there weren't any messages from him either.

The next weekend in the library, he came up to her and they talked for a few minutes. There was no explanation about why he hadn't called. He just walked up with this sexy gait and began weaving tales in the French accent, and Zel's body responded.

But he didn't call after that either. When he saw her in the quad, he spoke and always talked a few minutes. Even at the show they had once a week in the auditorium, he broke away from his friends to say a few nice words. Still he didn't call, and what really bugged Zel is that she asked him if he had lost her telephone number.

"Your number? No, I wrote in my date book. See? It's still here."

Zel would not lower herself to ask why he hadn't called. She figured that she'd find out sooner or later, but they were in the second semester and he still hadn't called. However, they met at the library every Sunday to study. Shelia thought maybe he just wanted to be friends. If that was the case, Zel would kill him. As it stood now, she was going to have to elevate her game. Apparently, brazen invitations didn't work with him.

So as much as it pained her, she became his friend. The very word caught in the back of her throat. She stopped pursuing— everyone. She made sure that she occasionally showed up in places where Jacques would be, but that was the extent of their relationship.

That was until the NAACP Ball. It was a huge fundraiser. It was so popular that alumni would come back to campus. She needed a date. Normally, she would have just asked Jacques. She was trying a different tactic. She wanted him to ask her.

It had been so long since she was on this side of the fence that she didn't know what to do. She was so used to taking the lead that the thought of following was completely foreign. So how do you get a man to ask you out?

Zel swallowed her natural instinct. She saw Jacques on the quad one day. She asked him if he was going to the ball. Naturally, he returned the inquiry.

"So you're going, no?"

"Actually, no. I don't have a date."

"Surely, dere iz someone to take you."

"No one has asked me yet."

"Dat's no a probleem for you, n'est pas?"

"Usually no. But …" Zel did her best to look sad and disappointed. Finally, he picked up the hint.

"No, don't look so sad. I'll take you. Don't worry."

"Really? That would be great."

Shelia

2003

Devon's law firm had rented the Shedd Aquarium for a formal gala celebrating its fiftieth year, and Shelia was required to attend. She hated these corporate functions. She preferred staying at home to dressing up and pretending to care about Devon's career.

But since Devon and Mother worked at the same law firm, it would be hard to explain why she didn't show up. So she pulled a dress out of her closet, threw it on, and headed out. Shelia merged onto I-55. Exiting onto Lake Shore Drive, she followed the signs to the Museum Campus.

Fortunately, Zel made sure her closet was full of exquisite numbers, some of which Zel designed herself. Zel hadn't trusted Shelia to dress herself since college. Scratch that. Zel had never trusted Shelia to dress herself. So she made sure to send over dresses that she knew Shelia could rock.

The deep blue, floor-length number she was wearing tonight

had classic lines. It had long sleeves and came up to her neck in front. However, the back was completely non-existent all the way down to a centimeter above the crack of her ass. If she swirled around, side slits revealed the top of her thighs. She had completed her outfit with diamond earrings, a sapphire ring, a silver clutch, and silver heels.

The dress was beautifully cut and would have been perfect if Shelia had bothered to tell Zel how much weight she had lost over the past month. Anyone could see each vertebrae protruding through her skin. Thankfully, with the firm's high-profile client base, there was no way she would be the skinniest woman in the room.

Shelia took a breath and alighted from the car, giving her keys to the valet. She hustled out of the heat into the entrance bordered on either side by an oceanarium, took her phone out of her purse, and called Devon to let her know she made it. Within two minutes, he was by her side. He looked at her and frowned.

She looked down at her outfit. It still looked good. She walked up to him and touched cheeks, their public greeting to each other. "What's wrong?"

"You look tired. All the makeup in the world can't hide your eyes. You need to get yourself together."

"Really? Is this the place to have that conversation?"

Devon clenched his jaw and guided her into the room He gave her the lowdown on the room early to ensure she talked to all the right people before leaving.

He gave her a glass of wine, which she would pretend to sip throughout the night. She wasn't that much of a drinker, and she'd have to drive herself home probably sometime after the dinner, which was scheduled to start at 7:00 p.m., so she wanted to be sure she was sober.

She usually left before 10:00 p.m.; Devon always stayed until the very end. It worked for them.

Shelia stood in the corner with her wine, contemplating the best way to work the room when she saw Mother. She was facing

Shelia, and the gentleman she was talking to had his back to Shelia. He was over six feet tall and had to be cute. Mother was gently touching his forearm, which made Shelia smile. Leave it to Mother to find a contender in this mass of people.

Shelia was about to move in to speak to her; if she didn't at some point this evening, she would never hear the end of it. As she began walking, her perspective began to change. There was something about this man that was distinctly familiar. When he laughed, Shelia almost dropped her drink.

She whipped her head around looking for an exit and high-tailed it into the bathroom. People were looking at her strangely, but giving her a path. She turned and looked over her shoulder one more time before hitting the bathroom door. Their eyes met; his mirroring the shock that had to be apparent in hers. Rick Whyte. She knew Chicago was too small to ignore him forever.

Shelia headed for a stall. She needed a moment—a private moment. She'd like to think the beating of her heart was the shock of seeing Rick again. However, the tingle in her belly had nothing to do with shock and everything to do with a memory. She had only had sex with two men in her life—Rick and Devon. She had heard stories about women who never had an orgasm in their lives. Thank God, she never had that problem. Even now her panties were getting wet from memory alone.

1997

Her mind wandered back to a night months after they met, Shelia found herself in a very pleasing position with Rick's weight on top of her. His weight had become a welcome addition, sometimes even a necessary one. Crazy thing was that a couple of months earlier, she couldn't imagine depending on a man like this, wanting him, needing him, but Rick sort of just slipped into her life. She wished he'd come over every night and sleep beside her. When she told him that, he laughed and said there wasn't that much restraint in the world. So more often than not, she slept alone.

Even that night as his lips teased hers to open and as his tongue caressed hers, Shelia knew that it would end soon. His hand began to gently knead her breasts, he slid down her body until he was on all fours and his mouth took over for his hands. Shelia gasped and arched. My God. Her twat was throbbing, her mouth was hanging open; she wanted more.

Shelia took Rick's head in her hands and tried to suffocate him with her breasts. She could feel him smile against her, but she didn't care. She wanted more. His mouth was so warm against her breast.

He began to nibble at her swollen nubs, sucking and pulling.

She reached down through the top of his jogging pants and pulled his member. It weighed heavy in her hand. She began to rub it up and down. She took her thumb and rotated it around the tip. Light moisture from him eased her finger's journey.

This time Rick was the one gasping. Shelia smiled.

He pulled himself back up to Shelia's face and began to kiss her again. This time the gentleness was gone; he was probing and demanding her attention, forcing the pace. His hand slid down into her unsnapped waistband and he rubbed her clit.

Shelia moaned, arched, and then pushed his hand away. "Wait. Stop. Stop."

Rick ceased his motions and hung his head sighing. He looked up with the one question in his eyes. He'd told her it would be her decision. Of course, he'd admitted that he'd try his best to influence it, but they wouldn't go any further until she said the word.

Shelia closed her eyes and Rick rolled-off her onto his side. Sheila could sleep like this for the rest of the night; but most likely, he'd get up in a few minutes and head back to his dorm room. Rick nestled his rear against her, and she played lightly with his back and then kissed the back of his T-shirt.

Shelia was still tingling; her panties weren't merely moist, but soaking wet; her breasts were throbbing to have Rick's lips worshipping them once more. Her mind had been overthrown and her body was calling the shots—and it was calling for Rick. She loved him. Full stop. Period. And she wanted him. Tonight.

Shelia reached around and began to play with Rick's twins. Rick pulled her hand back. "Stop it. Lia."

"Why?"

"Because we're not going to do anything."

"Why?" Shelia asked softly.

Rick turned. "What?"

Shelia bit the side of her bottom lip. She didn't exactly know how to say it. So she sat up on her elbows and kissed him, gently pressing her lips against his. She invaded his mouth with her tongue, staging a peaceful coup.

Her hand gently lifted his shirt over his head, and she threw it on the floor.

They were now separated, and he looked into her eyes. "I want you to be sure, Lia. I won't be able to go much further and stop."

Shelia smiled. "I love you."

Rick's eyes gazed at her. "Thank you."

Shelia looked confused. "What?"

"Just. Thanks. For that, for this. Thanks."

Rick released the final three buttons on Shelia's blouse, undid her front-closure bra, and pushed them off of her shoulders in one swift move.

They took stock of each other. Rick was slender, but well-muscled, with stomach muscles that Shelia couldn't help but touch, caress.

Rick took Shelia's hand and stood her up. He helped her shimmy her jeans and underwear off at the same time before he took off his jogging pants and underwear.

Shelia found a place on the floor to focus her attention.

"Lia, babe. You can look."

"I'm OK. Can't we just get under the covers?"

"Please, look at me. I happen to be amazed that I'm with the most beautiful woman on campus."

"Rick, apparently, you miss all those women who scream your name when you're running up and down the court."

"Apparently, you think I care about them. I don't know them. I know you, and I want you to look at me."

Shelia gazed up into Rick's eyes.

"Lia, I meant the rest of me."

Timidly, Shelia's eyes began to shift down. She had to muster her courage to look below the waist. She had felt there and felt the presence, but not actually looked. Shelia took a quick peek. "Rick can we, um, get under the covers now?"

Rick shook his head, pushed her back onto the bed and covered her body with his and began kissing her again, caressing her, fondling her. It was like he had a thousand hands.

Shelia was going crazy. She wanted him to have a thousand more. Her breasts wanted the attention, her lips begged for his kiss, her abdomen wanted to be caressed, her neck wanted to be licked. He was doing everything, and it was not enough and too much at the same time.

Rick began to stroke her clit. He licked the tips of his fingers and rubbed. The pleasure was coming in waves, building and building.

"Please Rick. I want you inside me."

Rick switched hands and used the other one to find his pants and protection in the pocket. He left her for a minute to apply the condom and then his pressure was back. He began to rub at her vaginal opening, which was slick and wet—slick, wet, and tight. He worked in one finger. There was a sharp intake of Shelia's breath when he worked the second one in. He stroked with the two fingers letting her get used to the intrusion until she began rocking against his hand. Then she started to purr.

"Come on, baby."

Shelia opened her eyes. "I want you. I want to come with you in me. I want us to come together."

Rick slid his body over Shelia's and began to probe her, but the minute his fingers left her, her opening all but closed again. Using his fingers to lead the way, he pushed again. He began gently rocking to ease the opening slowly. Again Shelia purred.

However, Rick wasn't making headway. "Baby, open your legs a bit more."

Shelia complied.

Rick began to stroke her a bit more and kiss her. He stroked her breast with one hand and used the other one to try to get her to accommodate his other stroke.

"It's OK, baby. I'm ready."

Rick began to enter with a bit more force, using his muscular legs to provide the necessary leverage to make his way inside of her.

Shelia gasped a bit, but it didn't stop her from wanting more. Suddenly, he sucked in his breath and bit off a curse.

Shelia opened her eyes and looked at him. "What happened, babe?"

"Nothing, honey. Everything is perfect. I just have to work it in a bit. You're tight."

"I'm sorry."

"Are you kidding? Don't apologize. You are giving me the greatest gift."

Rick began kissing her again. He maneuvered until he was on bottom and she was on top. "Ride me, baby."

Checking her readiness, he held his penis, while she tried to impale herself. She sat down on top of him and still felt resistance. Her body was not stretching to accommodate him.

"Rock a bit, baby."

Shelia began rocking, but instead of easing Rick into her, her body continued to resist. She tried to force it in and felt a little give at the same time Rick bit off another curse.

"What happened?"

"You just bent me a little, babe."

"Oh my God! It doesn't fit."

"Sssh. Baby, of course it will."

"No. No. It doesn't fit. It just doesn't fit." Shelia's eyes were wide, wild. She jumped off and started backing away, "I'm so sorry. Maybe there are some exercises I can do. I'm sorry. I just … It didn't fit."

"Lia, come here."

"No, umm. Maybe, maybe you should go back to your dorm room. Yeah. Umm. I don't understand. I'm sorry."

Rick stood up, deflated in a couple of areas. "Lia, babe. Come here." He walked over to her and wrapped his arms around her. They stood there rocking while her tears began to drop.

"Sshh, babe. Don't cry."

"Rick has this happened to you before? Tell me the truth."

"No, but that doesn't mean it's never happened before in life. Honestly, I don't have a lot of experience with virgins."

Shelia tore away from him. "I'm sure your women are very experienced. I'm just a sexual failure. I'm the first failure that I've ever heard of. Girls talk, you know. I've never heard a conversation that began with 'He couldn't get it in.' Let's just forget it."

"Forget what?"

"Forget all of this."

"No."

"Why? You apparently aren't going to get satisfaction from me." Shelia's eyes widened. "Wait. Come here."

Rick walked over to Shelia, and she immediately fell to her knees.

Rick jumped back and picked her up from the floor. "Babe, that generally isn't the consolation prize to sex."

"I want to please you. I love you."

"Then sleep with me. Just us. Like this. Getting our 'zees' on."

Rick looked Shelia in the eyes and began to smile a little. "Huh. What about that?"

"Are you sure?"

"We'll work our way around this. I promise, but we're not going to forget anything. What we have going on here is much too special to talk about forgetting anything. So we'll take this part really slow. It'll be worth it. Promise."

Rick led Shelia to the bed, pulled the cover over both of them, and hugged her until she fell asleep. He watched her for a while. He had no clue how they were going to work around how tight she was. This was the first time he had encountered anything like this, either by direct knowledge or through locker room lessons. As Rick drifted off to sleep, he had no clue how they were supposed to get through this. He was horny and really could use a bit of relief.

Shelia thought she was having the most delicious dream. Her breasts were being delicately nibbled. She stretched and turned from her side to her back. Her dream never felt this deliciously real. The mouth released her breast. She gave a disgruntled moan, but the next thing she knew a hand was caressing her soft, private folds. She smiled. This was the best … dream? Shelia frowned. This was too good. Too real.

She opened her eyes and saw Rick staring at her. She stretched and moaned again.

"Whoo, babe. It's still dark. What time is it?"

"Late. Early. Depending on how you look at it."

"Oh, yeah. Oh." Shelia slowly inhaled and twisted her body to give Rick easier access. "God that feels too good."

Shelia was caught somewhere between dream and reality. It felt surreal, but phenomenal. She pushed her pelvis into Rick's hands. She was slick, and his fingers were working magic. Rick began to reach over her.

"No, don't stop."

"Lia, I'm just going to get …"

Shelia grabbed his hand and placed it where it was. "Don't stop."

"But, I need—"

Shelia opened her eyes and looked at him. "You only need me."

She began kissing him. Her hot, moist mouth followed her hands everywhere on his body. Her tongue performed tricks on his chest that had him standing staunchly at attention. So much so that he was actually tapping her belly with his staff. Shelia smiled and looked Rick in the eye when she began to move down and give his staff the attention that it deserved. She opened her mouth and deep-throated it.

Rick's shout of "Ooh, baby, damn" and the fact that he was stroking her mouth told her she was doing something right. Shelia took her tongue and swirled it around his tip then, she started near the base and licked her way up. She took him fully in her mouth again and began to move her head up and down.

Rick began to squirm a bit. She heard his sharp breaths, his moans, groans. His reaction made her even more anxious to have him inside her. She was dripping on the sheets, and he was obviously ready. She sat up.

Rick begged her with his eyes and voice, "Please baby don't stop."

Shelia merely looked into his eyes, took him in her hand, nestled him in her hot folds, and began to rock.

"Shelia, baby. We can't. Ooh shit. We need to get something." But then Shelia's body began to accept him. Each rock opened her a little more. Each push got him further inside. He tried for a minute to pull out of her and push his rear into the mattress.

Soon he was contributing to her deflowering. He was meeting each rock of hers with a thrust of his own. Then he was completely inside, and neither one of them was thinking about anything else but, the pleasure they were finding. Each had their own intakes of breath, moans. Their sweat mingled with each other's. The feelings generated were too much. Then Rick reached down and started playing with

Shelia's clit.

It was too much. She erupted and convulsed around Rick.

Rick soon gave in to his own pleasure, and with a few more strokes found his own release.

Shelia woke for the second time that Sunday morning with Rick staring into her eyes.

2003

Shelia brought herself back to reality: she was hiding in the bathroom at a company function. She had already been in there longer than could be explained by anything, but Montezuma's revenge. Her skin felt hot to touch, from memory alone. She was damn near sweating. That might actually work in her favor for a sick excuse.

She flushed the toilet for appearance's sake and washed her hands. She looked at herself critically in the mirror. Devon was right. Those bags were hard to miss. She had yet to find a cover-up that did more than make them more pronounced.

While Shelia freshened her makeup, she let the memories come back. It was better for them to appear here, while she was alone in the bathroom, than when she was standing across from Rick. She hadn't seen him since a barbecue that fateful summer that she found out she was pregnant. She never told him. She didn't even tell Zel until they were already in Paris.

Shelia took a deep breath, checked her dress, and walked out. She felt Rick's eyes on her as she navigated the room. She smiled and talked to all the people on Devon's list. Rick was not on it, so she figured she'd save their encounter for as late as she possibly could.

She felt him in different places in the room, but he didn't come over to say anything. She couldn't fault him for that. One minute they're in love. The next minute she's writing him a Dear John letter, which he would have gotten after she was already on the plane. If he had done that to her, she would have gotten a voodoo doll and put roots on him.

She thought it was for the best. She wouldn't have been able to see him and not tell him about the baby. This man who was trying to make a way for his whole family would have tried to do "right" by her, whatever that would have meant. At what cost?

She wasn't new. She knew where babies came from. She knew she was taking a huge risk, after that first time, to have sex without a condom again. However, she thought she was safe. They had been loosey goosey with protection for months. The only shock there should have been was the fact that it didn't happen that first month.

Shelia tried to concentrate on small talk, when all she wanted to do was jet out the door, jump in her car, and hide out at home. As the staff announced dinner, Shelia and Devon reconnected to sit at their designated table. He leaned over, "Are you OK? If possible, you look worse than you did when you first came in."

Shelia rolled her eyes. A man of tact, he was not. "I'm getting a migraine, but I'll be OK." Shelia smiled and touched his forearm. The forearm trick was a secret she had learned by watching Mother. Devon nodded and started conversing with other tablemates.

Shelia was glad when the food arrived, so that she could concentrate on that instead of trying to come-up with more conversation. She was sitting next to the fifty-year-old wife, of a hundred-year-old man. Nothing about that situation sounded right. Not only that, but when she tried to talk to the wife she quickly realized that she needed to use words simple enough for a Dr. Seuss book. Shelia figured the lady was the trophy wife "back in the day." That day had truly passed.

Shelia remembered her mother told her it was one thing to be old. It was another thing to look old. However, at the time, she was only referring to the fact that "Dark and Lovely" was a staple in their house, like milk and eggs. Shelia hoped her plastic surgeon had a frequent visitor card or something: Get two face lifts, get a nose job free.

Shelia would have to tell Zel about this. She'd get a kick

out of it. Speaking of which, she hadn't spoken with Zel in a while. Shelia would have to call her to check in. She continued to smile as she endured the wife's conversation about her latest trip to some hot island. It was unfortunate that her husband's health did not permit him to go. Shelia almost guffawed. Almost. She let her thoughts entertain her through dinner. It didn't take a whole lot of brain power to keep-up with the wife's conversation.

By the time the speeches and entertainment ended, it was close to 9:00 p.m. The band began playing. Shelia figured she could make her exit at any point.

Devon grabbed her up quickly. He knew her well enough to figure she was planning her exit strategy. They danced for a bit and talked about nothing. As he was about to walk her to the door, he was waylaid by one of the partners. Instead of staying with him, she told him she'd see him at home and headed down to get her car.

She gave her ticket to the valet and stood in line with the others. She noticed Rick fine, and dateless, also waiting on his car.

He turned around. "Hey Lia."

"Hey, Rick."

"It's been a while."

"Umm, yes."

"So you're married to Devon Sims. I've heard good things about him."

"Thanks. And the Bulls made it to the playoffs this year. Congratulations. You really helped them off of the bench."

"You follow basketball like that?"

Shelia laughed. "No, but it's the Bulls. In Chicago, you'd have to be a hermit. No. You'd have to be dead not to hear commentary someplace. I'm only repeating, but the guy sounded like a reliable source."

Rick smiled. That smile still made Shelia's mind go into overdrive. Who was she kidding? It was her body telling her mind to do all sorts of inappropriate things.

"Thanks. I appreciate that, even if it's a second-hand accounting. I don't know how to ask this, so please don't take it the wrong way, but have you been ill? You don't look to well."

Shelia swore to herself that she was going to befriend men with tact one of these days. At least he apologized, beforehand. "I'm fighting a migraine. That's all."

Rick looked skeptical, but simply said, "Well, here's my car. Maybe we can catch up sometimes. Devon is welcome to join of course. I don't want to get caught in any domestic situation." He handed her a card.

"Yeah, it would be great to catch up."

Shelia watched Rick get in his car and drive off.

Soon her vehicle was in front of her, and she made her way home. She couldn't delay. No matter what time it was in Paris, she needed to talk to Zel tonight.

AYAAN

It had taken Kendall forever to settle down for the night. She wanted to hear story after story. Ayaan kept obliging. Reading to Kendall occupied her mind. All the way home, all she could think about was how good Kenneth looked. The only difference in all these years was his eyes. While she used to be able to read every thought and emotion, now he shuttered them, only allowing a glimpse into what he was thinking.

Eventually, Ayaan put an end to storytelling and closed the door. Kendall would go on forever with an audience. Sometimes she went on forever without an audience. Ayaan could hear her singing to herself. Eventually, she'd sing herself to sleep.

Kendall was unaware that her room was still wired. Ayaan wasn't comfortable without being able to hear what was going on in there. Kendall was adamant that she was a big girl and didn't need a monitor. Matter of fact, Kendall refused to lie down for naps while the monitor was still in her room.

Ayaan made a big production of removing the monitor only to go back in and hide it later. Her friends told her that she was going to have trouble with Kendall later, if she kept giving in to her now. Ayaan didn't have any problems. Kendall loved to please and make people happy. It was rare for her not to do what Ayaan told her.

The problem wasn't listening. It was interpreting. Case in point, Kendall was so proud that she learned her phone number and address that she started telling them to perfect strangers. She'd tell them to people in the grocery store, in the park, parents' of children at school. She even told a police officer that came to their school to talk to the children once, that if she ever got lost that she knew what to do and proceeded to tell him all of her information.

At that point, Ayaan put her foot down and proceeded to give Kendall strict instructions on when to tell her number and address.

Now, Kendall didn't tell her information to everyone. As evidenced by her story about the park, Kendall just told people how to get to their house. She specifically did not give out her phone number and address. Ayaan was going to have to be quick to keep ahead of her daughter.

Ayaan poured a glass of wine and took the monitor receiver to the front porch. She loved sitting on her step on warm nights, especially after she found a bug repellent that actually worked. Now she could listen to the quiet of the block at night. She did have quite a bit of work to do, but she'd caffeinate herself back up later. Now was her time.

Kendall was still singing to herself, but occasionally that was broken by a yawn. Ayaan would give her ten minutes tops before she went to sleep. The benefit of living in this neighborhood was that even though this was Friday night, there wasn't anyone out disturbing her peace. It felt good.

Ayaan was glad she'd seen Kenneth today. She knew logically that there wasn't anything she could do about Shelia moving in next door. She was just a bit put off that Shelia had unilaterally decided to move in without so much as a heads-up. Then, when Shelia moved in, she didn't so much as say a peep to Ayaan. How rude was that? It took the one person who connected them both to force the discussion. Of course, Ayaan couldn't say it was much of a discussion because nothing was actually settled. However, at least they spoke.

The other thing that was really poking at Ayaan was guilt. Shelia didn't look well. She had seen her after having gone through hours of labor and delivering her child. A woman looks rough after that. Shelia looked stronger *then*. The years hadn't been kind to her. There didn't seem to be any strength left in her. Shelia seemed deflated, a shell.

Kendall was right. Ayaan had been watching Shelia, and maybe she had made a few comments to Cleo. They were accurate. That girl seemed to be holding onto sanity with fingers as slippery as chicken grease. That was not good. It was another layer that Ayaan had to figure out. She had to figure out what to tell Kendall about Shelia. However, Shelia had her own issues to deal with right now. How could she have not told anyone that she gave her baby up for adoption? That's major. So Ayaan was at Shelia's mercy—at least up to this point.

Ayaan sipped on her wine. She guessed Shelia had a different relationship with Devon than Ayaan had with Kenneth. There wasn't an aspect of her life that he didn't know by the time they got together. With her parents' deaths, Ayaan didn't have anyone else. So when Kenneth came along, she reveled in the closeness of their relationship. There was an unexplained intimacy of sharing all your deepest fears and secrets under the cover of a dark room. They did.

One fact that she religiously kept from every guy she dated was one that Kenneth already knew. Ayaan had uterine fibroids. For a while, it was manageable. She seemed to be on her period all the time and sometimes experienced cramps. That was it until the week she got her period. That loss of blood led to low iron. Then she was like Niagara

Falls. She would bleed heavily and her iron levels would drop. It wasn't really what they discussed over coffee. However, when she passed out while they were working out at the gym, it was obvious that something was a bit off. Until that point, she just worked with the fibroids.

One minute she was alternating push-ups and sit-ups. The next minute she was being shaken awake. She had passed out before, so she wasn't as freaked out as the people in her workout class. Of course, she hadn't passed out for that long before. Next thing she knew, someone was shoving a nutrition bar under her nose. Kenneth helped her to the front of the gym, where an ambulance was pulling up. They pricked her finger and checked her blood levels.

Ayaan was mortified. Kenneth looked scared. He actually took it upon himself to go with her to the doctor. Both of her doctors knew about her condition. So they weren't surprised that she fainted. This time, though, they both were recommending surgery. The problem with surgery was they couldn't guarantee that they'd be able to save her uterus. That unknown was the scariest part. She couldn't imagine anything worse than going into surgery with a seventy-eight percent success rate and waking up to find she was in the other twelve percent.

When she woke up from surgery, Kenneth was sleeping as comfortably as he could in a chair, wearing a T-shirt with two arrows. The one pointing to his face said, "The man." The one pointing to his dick said, "The Legend." She laughed silently—only him. She prayed it was a gift. Who would buy something like that? She figured if he had to brag about it, there probably wasn't much to brag about.

Ayaan tried to sit up a bit. The moan that escaped her lips woke Kenneth.

"How do you feel?"

"Great. Everyone should have people poking about in their insides. Why did they let you stay?"

"I refused to leave."

"Hmm. Afraid that I gave your half of the business to your mother in my will?" That's the last thing she remembered saying.

Kenneth swore they had a longer conversation, but he also said that she promised to cook for him for staying with her in the hospital.

Ayaan shook her head. She was never so drugged as to promise to cook anyone anything. She was too busy trying to find a man who would cook for her. For the first day, Ayaan was in and out of consciousness. She vaguely remembered friends, doctors, and nurses stopping by, but they blurred together.

The next day when the doctor was doing his rounds he gave her the news—and it wasn't good. They gave her a complete hysterectomy. She'd never have children. With that, Ayaan broke down in a way she hadn't since her parents died.

Her body healed. However, the thought of never having children wore her mind to a nub. She couldn't do her job anymore, because every time she left the house, there were children. There were parents. She'd never have that. All she would have was an empty shell where a child was supposed to grow.

Bearing children was one of the greatest things a woman could do. She felt like such a failure. She had succeeded so much in life that she didn't know how to deal with failure. So she shut down. She didn't talk to friends. She didn't talk to anyone. She didn't do anything, but sit around her house. She was in bed every night by 8:30 p.m. She would have gone to bed earlier, but she felt that would be pretty pathetic. She woke up every day, took a shower, cried, ran a few errands, cried, watched some television, cried, and went to bed crying herself to sleep.

Kenneth found temporary help. He covered all of her speaking engagements, even the ones to women's entrepreneurial groups. He stopped by once a day to make sure she was still breathing, until he got good and pissed for her leaving him alone to do the work. Then things got real—quickly.

Kenneth folded his arms and asked, "Are you done yet?"

"Leave me alone," Ayaan answered as she glared at him.

"No."

She tried again. "Just go away."

"No."

Ayaan had a limited amount of time that she could actually talk to people before she broke down crying again. Kenneth crossed that line and still refused to leave.

"Listen, we have got work to do. We have a business to run. We have lives to lead. You aren't dead, but I'm seconds from clocking you out. I don't care if you cry in front of every single client we have from now until infinity. You are going to do your job. You owe me."

"I don't owe you—"

"The minute you signed on to be my business partner you made a promise. And I'm not letting you out of it. Two weeks. You've had two weeks. That's all you get from me."

He took her to dinner first. She supposed it was to test the water. Kenneth sat at the table and continued his conversation around her tears. Thinking about it now, it must have looked crazy as hell—him chatting away and her constantly wiping her eyes. The next time got easier. The time after that got a bit easier. There were still times when she would look at a child and ache, but she realized that she could survive.

There was a certain freedom in not worrying about biological clocks. Kenneth always said he avoided dating older women without children because they were on the fast track to marriage and kids. Younger women took it easy. Ayaan stayed on her own track. She went out and had fun. She never even thought of men in the forever sense. She thought about them in the "for now" sense. That was, of course, before she got together with Kenneth.

In a lot of ways, that too was based on the fact that she didn't want to have to explain to men that she couldn't have children. She hadn't told one man that she dated after the surgery that she couldn't have children. It wasn't their business. So she became a party girl and enjoyed the life that she was dealt.

Ayaan ran her hand over her face. She wasn't surprised to

find tears. Even now, with Kendall sleeping soundly in the bedroom upstairs, she felt a little a twinge about the fact that she couldn't have produced Kendall.

She noticed Shelia's car come up the block and turn into the driveway. As upset as she was wit hShelia, she knew that she could pretend as much as she wanted; but in truth, Kendall was Shelia's biological child. They had an open adoption arrangement. While she would have preferred for it to be more defined in the beginning, it wasn't completely untenable. She had to take charge. Obviously, Shelia was in no shape.

Ayaan was again thankful to Kenneth. She knew depression. She understood it as few people did. She saw the dark side of her mind and how it could take control until there was little to no light getting through, but she had someone to drag her out kicking and screaming. It seemed to her that Shelia functioned well enough, but she probably hadn't lived since she handed over her daughter.

Shelia always looked like her survival was held together by a spidery web; anything could send her the rest of the way around the bend. Then she wouldn't be good for anyone.

Ayaan finished her glass of wine. She would call her lawyer in the morning and draw up some new custody papers. If she was going to tackle this, it was going to have to be head-on with a ruthless determination; sort of like Kenneth when he sat across from her in the restaurant pretending she wasn't a bawling mess. That took guts.

This issue with her neighbor was only going to work if they had a plan. Ayaan was going to drive that plan. She had to. Kendall's happiness was at stake—and she'd shank a bitch before she'd let anyone steal Kendall's happiness.

Shelia

2003

It was about 5:00 a.m. in Paris. This was probably the best time to call Zel, but something held her back. She knew she was now treading on dangerous ground. Zel wanted her to move back to Paris and work for her. She wanted Shelia to leave Devon, ignore their promise; and hop on a plane to another country. At one point, that's just what she did. That's how she got into this situation that she was in now. She merely hopped on a plane.

1997

What do you do when you're nineteen and the stick turns blue? Shelia had taken three pregnancy tests, and they all showed the same thing. She was pregnant. She knew anyway. Her breasts were sore. She was tired all the time. She kept a queasy stomach. She knew before she went to the drugstore. She had spent the day loitering here and there. Time was something she didn't have. When Rick found out, his whole life would change; she couldn't let that happen. No matter what, he couldn't find out. He was much too grown, too responsible.

So she did the only thing she could think of, she went to talk to Zel. Shelia rang Zel's bell and waited.

"Hey, Lia."

Zel's arresting face was tragically composed. Lashes spiked by tears making them even more pronounced—lips pouting with the struggle to keep in the cry that was trying to fight its way through choppy breaths.

Shelia walked into the foyer and opened her arms, Zel fell into them and let out the heart-wrenching sobs that were lying just below the surface.

Mama T got up from her perch on the overstuffed cream chair. She walked over to hug Shelia. "Thank you so much for coming."

Shelia looked a bit perplexed. "What's going on?"

Mama T looked back and forth from Shelia to Zelphia. "I thought Zel called you for you to come over."

Zel rolled her eyes up to the ceiling, "I never quite got around to calling her."

"Doesn't matter, must be kismet. Why don't you two come and have a seat and talk?"

"Zel, sweetie, what happened?"

Zel looked at Shelia's concerned face. She was sure her face looked a wreck. Zel didn't know how to begin. So she figured she'd start at the end. One would think that was the easiest part, but having to say the words out loud was almost more than she could bear. She took a deep breath and opened her mouth. It was like actually saying the words would validate what happened. Not saying them wouldn't take it back, but she didn't know if she had the strength. So she started a little earlier than the end.

"Did I ever tell you about the last night Jacques and I spent together? I doubt it; the semester was over and you had already left for home."

"That night, he rented a hotel room. He had to. The dorms were closed and he had gotten this great deal on a plane ticket, but he had to leave on Tuesday. So he asked me to stay. Mama T had already taken my stuff home. So I stayed.

"He was his usual romantic self—candlelight, wine (good wine too). That man could pick a good bottle of wine as easily as breathing. Full-bodied, because I prefer it. He had this gift-wrapped box. Not a ring box, but definitely jewelry. I was so excited. He made me wait until after this great dinner. Man, he threw down in that kitchen. Then he made me wait until after dessert. All the while, this box is in the middle of the table calling my name. You know how impatient I can be." Zel smiled a bit, a really sad smile.

She started the story again. This time her voice wasn't as strong. It began to crack, and she cleared her throat and started over. "By the time dinner was over, I was almost leaping out of my seat. So he gave me this box and told me that I would always have a piece of his heart."

Zel leaned forward to show Shelia this delicate platinum chain and charm. The charm was a circle with delicate webbing. It had feather-shaped attachments hanging from the bottom of the charm.

Zel leaned back and gazed at the charm. "He told me it was a dream-catcher. He said that I embodied every dream that he ever had, and he wanted to give me something that would remind me of what I meant to him. He told me that I was phenomenal. He loved my mind, my sarcasm, my sassiness, my intelligence and my strength. He told me he loved all those things about me, Shelia. He told me that whatever I wanted to do, I would succeed. He wanted me to throw out a dream and go for it.

"Then he kissed me." Zel picked up her hand that was gently shaking and she pointed to the places where Jacques had kissed—"on my forehead, my cheek, my neck. He drew me up into his arms and we danced. I didn't spend the night. I had a slice of perfection. I didn't want anything to spoil it. So I kissed one cheek, then the other. And I inhaled his scent as I hugged him good-bye and I left."

"Zel, sweetheart, that was over a month ago."

"Yeah, yeah. It was."

She licked her bottom lip, and with her back turned, she continued her story. "Jacques decided that he wanted to backpack around Europe this summer. It was no big deal. He got together with some friends and hit the road. They had done it the summer before and had a blast. You know Jacques's parents financed his whole summer. Well, anyway. I got to talk to him pretty regularly. I made him describe everything to me. I swear I thought he was wasting his mind in business. He should have been a writer or something. It almost felt like I was seeing these places myself.

"Regardless of everything else, he promised to call every Thursday morning at 8:00 a.m. my time. My day to call was Monday. That way we'd at least talk twice a week. Well, he didn't call. So I called him and talked with one of his friends."

"He's …," Zel turned. Misery was drawing her lips down into a frown. "He was always so playful, you know."

Shelia's eyes began to tear-up and a weight began to settle over her heart in anticipation of the next words.

"So they were running around playing like kids and he was too close to the street. When he tripped, he couldn't stop his fall. A car was passing another one just a bit too close to the curb."

Shelia covered her mouth with her hand and stared with horror at the tale Zel was spinning for her.

"He couldn't quite break his fall or jump back or anything. One minute he was smiling and the next minute —"

"Is he going to be OK?"

"He's going to be wonderful. Just not on the same plane that we are."

"Zel!"

"Shelia, his friends ... they didn't know what to say. His parents took custody of his remains. That's what they call them, right? Remains? The rest of his life is fulfilled through death."

Shelia walked to Zel and drew her into her arms. The tears were flowing, but not with the wracking sobs that she had earlier—but, the pain.

Zel began a moan that came from the epicenter of pain and radiated outward washing that pain over everyone in the immediate vicinity.

Shelia felt the pain with a tightening of her gut and tried to rock some of it out with Zel, but this pain would be there for a while.

"Shelia, I feel as if my heart is being ripped out piece by piece."

Zel glanced over at Mama T, who was crying for her daughter's broken heart. Zel mouthed, I love you, Mama.

Mama joined them in a group hug; each one trying to give and receive comfort; each one clueless on how to move forward, what to say next, what to do.

Zel was the one who broke the group hug and went over to the overstuffed chair that Mama T had vacated. Mama T and Shelia sat side by side on the couch.

Mama T looked at Shelia, "Do you want something to drink? I'd ask Zel, but she's threatened me if I try to pour anymore tea down her throat."

Shelia nodded, "Yes, I'd like whatever you have and ... I sorta need to talk to Zel. You know, if you don't mind."

Mama T looked at her indulgently, "not at all. Holler when you're ready for your drink."

Shelia looked at Zel. "Zel, sweetie - I need to ask you a couple of questions. They may be in poor taste, but I just need to know. Why did you and Jacques decide to wait until you had sex?"

"Please, I didn't have any role in that decision. Jacques decided to wait until we had sex."

"But why? I mean no offense, but you seemed to ... umm ...

really want to."

"Funny thing is that I know I pushed him about sex and made a big deal about wanting to be with him and lamented over and over again about not being with him, but I couldn't love him without respecting him and I respected his diligence—if that's the right word—regarding sex. And I didn't want to be the one to bring him down. OK," Zel said with a slight smirk, "maybe I did a little, but I learned just being with him was enough—even if I couldn't be *with* him.

"It's funny, but out of all the men I've run through, he's the only one I slowed down with long enough to know."

Shelia looked at Zel. "I don't mean to be macabre, but how does it feel? I mean I know it hurts, but you formed such a tight bond in such a short amount of time. What does it feel like?"

Zel looked at Shelia. "I want to call him and tell him so that he can comfort me. It's like I've lost my crutch. I survived without him. I don't know how I survived before, but I did. He was like a piece of the puzzle that just fit.

It wasn't that Barbie and Ken cutesy stuff. He didn't finish my sentences or want to dress alike. He wanted to know how I thought. How I acted. He wanted to know what made me tick. He made me question myself. It was fun at the time, but I wanted to make the transition into the woman I would become. He showed me that.

"To lose him … right now I can't get past the pain of the empty hole that he left in my life. I can't think past the pain of the thought that I can't talk to him anymore, laugh with him anymore, share with him anymore. I don't know how this will feel tomorrow, next week, next month. I just know that right now I'm just trying to make it from this minute, this second to the next—and that itself, is taking more strength than I knew I had."

Shelia took a long look at Zel. "Then let's go."

Zel looked puzzled. "Go where?"

"Let's go to France. Fine, you won't get to go to the funeral …" Shelia walked over and crouched down in front of Zel. "But you'll be able to say good-bye. You'll be able to see the places he told you about. You'll be able to have a part of his life. We won't be gone for long. School will start soon enough, but … it'll give you … It feels right."

Zel cocked her head to the side as she contemplated Shelia's offer.

"I can't do that alone. I'm not strong enough."

"You could, Zel. You're the strongest person that I know, but you won't have to. I'll go with you."

Zel actually laughed out loud. "Girl, please."

"Seriously, Zel; Mother made me get a passport in case my "meant to be" wanted to travel unexpectedly. Gosh, that woman lives in a fairytale world."

Zel's sad face had the beginning of a smirk. "Are you sure? It won't be pretty when Mother finds out."

"Sweetie," Shelia said with her hand on the side of Zel's face. "I'm sure."

Zel leaned into Shelia's hand.

"But Zel, I hope you can finance this trip because we both know I'm broke."

Zel smiled and nodded.

Zel didn't even know Shelia was pregnant when she left home. OK, ran from home. She used Zel's need to say goodbye to Jacques as an excuse. Zel was a wreck on the plane ride over, but she had actually perked up when they landed. She dragged an exhausted Shelia around to a couple of her favorite stores, but Zel came crashing down again once they reached the room.

Shelia could hear Zel's fractured breathing patterns; and although sleep was doing its best to pull her under, Shelia asked, "Is there anything I can do to make it better?"

"What did Rick say when you left? I bet that was a parting for the papers. The way you two are in each other's orbits."

Shelia was silent. One question would lead to two, two to four.

She knew that this conversation would come eventually. She was not prepared for this soon.

"I'm sure he understood."

"You're sure he understood. Why don't you know whether or not he understood?"

"I sort of left him a note."

"I know we left in a hurry. I didn't know you didn't have time to say goodbye. Call him now. I'll pretend not to listen."

"I might have broken up with him in the letter."

"I'm too tired to ask why you did that. Call him and undo it. We'll be back soon enough."

"I can't."

"You loved him. I saw it. I mean every time I looked at you two or were around you two, I knew it was right."

"I'm learning loving someone sometimes is not enough to make all your problems go away."

"But you could share them and work through them together."

"Well, sometimes it isn't that kind of party."

"See, I'm sitting here pining over a man that was yanked from me. I would have fought shit. I would have fought to the fucking, umm ummm, damnit to the pain for him."

Shelia looked confused for a minute. All this could mean is Zel was pissed beyond reason. When she was too mad to think of her own words, she used her random collection of memorized movie quotes.

"Yeah, you guys were a great fit."

"I enjoyed myself before him, and I have no regrets with the life I led, but being with him changed me. It wasn't even that he asked me to change. He was resistant to our relationship. You know that. Hell, the whole quad knew that, but it was like other men fell off the face of the earth.

"I would go to parties and some guy would try to pick me up. And it was like, ugh, back off. The guy would be fine and have a hell of a body and all that, but he wasn't Jacques. No one else even held my interest."

"Zel, I can imagine this is very hard for you. I know you loved him."

"Yeah, I did—and see, that's what I just don't understand. I didn't have a choice. You did, and you left Rick. Jacques was ripped from me. That was not my decision, but you, you toss love away like a fucking old sock. Like you believe love just comes sauntering around the corner every day. Oh look—love. Welcome."

"Listen, it wasn't easy, but it was for the best. You think I don't know how good I had it? You think I don't know that I may never have it that good again? You think I don't get that? Oh, I get it more than you know."

"How could you lose the one man that made you reach 'for the best'?"

"Right now, let's just concentrate on you."

"No, I want to know. How are you going to survive Rick, because I sure as hell don't know if I'm going to survive Jacques? If you can just walk away, I need to know how. How do you let that go? How do you get on with your life? How do you get out of bed in the morning? How do you make yourself get moving? What is your motivation? Because mine is to get to Jacques—living, dead it doesn't matter."

Shelia began to withdraw, but Zel was on a rampage. Zel could care less for the tears streaming out of Shelia's eyes or the fear in her face. Zel needed answers, and she was hell-bent on getting them. "How Shelia? How did you do it? Tell me. Tell me."

Shelia sat up, grabbing the pillow in front of her and began rocking.

Shelia tried to explain. "He deserved better."

Ayaan snorted. "Bullshit."

She tried a different approach. "I wanted to be here for you."

Ayaan merely shook her head. "Don't bullshit me. I don't know why you're here, but it's clearly not for me. You were running away.

Even from the great all powerful Mother, you ran away. How could you let him go?"

"I didn't have a choice."

"You had a choice."

"He had no future with me."

"You were his damn future."

"Basketball was his future—his future—his family's future. I couldn't take that away."

"Why did you have to? You loved him. He loved you. He could love you and play basketball. How do you willingly walk away from the one man who would have loved you forever?" Zel was shouting and crying; her face was covered with mucus that she carelessly brushed away with the back of her hand. "How could you? You were his future, dammit. You were his future."

Very quietly, rubbing her stomach, Shelia whispered, "But our baby was not. Our baby would have ruined his scholarship. He would have done everything in his power to take care of us, but what would that have meant to him?"

Shell-shocked, Zel retreated into the corner of the room and sat on her haunches with her head hanging down.

Shelia continued. "He was all they had. They were risking everything to get him to succeed. I couldn't derail his dream, his family's dream."

Zel looked. "He doesn't know? Do you have the right to make that decision for him?"

Shelia got off of her bed and walked over to Zel. "Absolutely not; I don't have the right to make that decision for him, but I don't have a choice."

"He'll find out when we go back to school in the fall."

"That's another thing. I'm not going back. I'm staying here at least until the baby is born, and then I'll think about my options."

Zel's eyes widened to twice the size of her face.

Shelia watched as the pieces began to fall into place.

Zel's lips opened into a round "O." "You never planned on going home."

"I had some tough decisions to make. When I burned that bridge with Rick, I couldn't risk him finding out."

"You're only here to run away from Rick."

"No, I'm here because the best friend I have in the world needed me to be here. Although I knew I was going to hide out, I never dreamed of hiding out in Paris. I never dreamed of dragging you into this. I had hoped to make it through your mourning and send you home alone."

"He would have stuck by you."

"I know."

"You should have told him. Even now," Zel reiterated with tears streaming down her face. "I still don't understand how you could have walked away."

"Well. Felt right at the time, and there's no turning back now."

"I would have fought like hell to have it all."

Shelia gave her a half smile. She believed with every bone in her body that Zel would have fought to have it all. She probably would have succeeded, too. No matter how many times Shelia went over this in her mind, the end result always seemed to be Rick dropping out of college to take care of his family. No college. No basketball. No basketball, no NBA. Shelia knew he was that good. He'd never get the chance to show it, working at some bootlegged job. Zel would have worked it out. "Yeah, you would have."

With that, they helped each other into bed. Zel still looked at Shelia with disbelief at times, but soon they drifted off into a sleep coma that they didn't wake up from until twelve hours later.

Shelia and Zel spent their first two days in Paris, alternatively sleeping and crying until Zel managed to get up the courage to go to the corner where Jacques died. Then two days after that, Zel slept and then she firmly stated,

"I'll stay here with you."

"I don't want you to."

"I need to be here for a while."

Shelia hung her head and nodded, but mentally she battled with herself. The last thing Shelia needed was for Zel to stay. Shelia had made a decision, too. She couldn't take the baby back to Chicago. Both Mother and Rick were there.

2003

The ringing of the phone brought Shelia back to the present. She checked the caller ID and picked it up. "Wow! Are you psychic?"

"No, I just got an interesting e-mail. Is Devon around?"

"No, he's at the company party. I won't see him for about another hour."

"So you saw Rick tonight."

"Yeah, when I first saw him, I ran straight for the bathroom and barricaded myself in."

Zel let out a surprised laugh. "No."

"Yes." Shelia giggled a bit. "I wasn't prepared for that."

"You know he's in Chicago. Why aren't you prepared to see him?" Zel asked.

Shelia shrugged. "I was at an office party. Why would I think that he would be there?"

"I guess. How did he look?"

Shelia replied to Zel. "You've seen him over the years. You know how he looks."

Zel smirked. "True, but I want to know what you think."

Sighing, Shelia responded. "Girl, you know he's still fine."

"Did you get the tingle?"

"Married, remember."

"Alive, remember."

Shelia thought about it. Of course she got the tingle, but she wasn't telling Zel that. That's something you kept to yourself.

"He told me that we should meetu p for a meal. He invited Devon."

"Girl, don't do it. You never get the old guy and the new guy together, especially when you loved the old guy to pieces and merely tolerate the new guy."

"It wasn't romantic or anything. There weren't any violins playing when we talked. It was just a conversation. It felt good. We were good friends at one point."

"You were fucking at one point. Don't pretend you guys were shooting hoops together on the playground. That was your man, not your boy."

Shelia thought about what Zel was saying. Her nuances were sharpshooter-accurate. However, just because he was her man once, things were different now. They both had moved on. He was doing well in the pros. She had Devon. Shelia tilted her head. That didn't seem to equate, but her life wasn't horrible. She did alright.

Fine, he ended up with his college degree. Shelia never went back to school. He ended up going to the pros. Shelia was a stay-at-home—well, nothing really. She just stayed at home. She actually had a cleaning lady come in a couple of times a week to keep the house spotless.

She did run errands. So she was more of a stay-at-home administrative assistant. Crap. It sounded like an empty life, no matter how you cut it. She thought about it a bit. She should at least volunteer. Now, she didn't know how she spent her days. Time went on. That's all she knew.

Zel changed the subject and went on to talk about her "mood board" for next year's collection. She was excited about the fabrics that she was going to work with. Shelia knew automatically that Zel would create one look specifically for her. She always did. Shelia listened with half an ear until she heard the garage door rattle.

"Devon's home. Let me talk to you later."

Zel

2003

Zel looked at her cell phone. Of course! Shelia had to go. Shelia always had to go. Zel swore every week that she was going to get a new best friend. She had new friends, of course. She was in Paris. She had to have new friends. Still no one knew her as well as Shelia did, even though she was perennially absent. However, for the most part, Shelia was an absentee friend. There were Parisian vendors that knew more about Zel's personal life now than Shelia did. Once in a while, though, Shelia would pay attention and give Zel a piece of insight that reminded Zel of the old Shelia—the BP (before Paris) Shelia. That's the Shelia that Zel missed.

That Shelia was fun. The Shelia who had loved Rick fully as only first love can manage, was Zel's best friend. Zel remembered when they used to go out together—Shelia, Rick, Zel, and Jacques.

Those were the days. Jacques, Zel's first love, the reason any of them landed in Paris at all.

Zel smiled, remembering how she pursued Jacques with a single-minded determination. He was just as determined to remain elusive. It forced her to learn about him. She delved into his life more deeply than she had anyone's in the past. At first, it was definitely the gorgeous smile and the accent that kept her coming back; though after she learned about him, it was his heart that kept her by his side. That first year in Paris was the most emotional of Zel's life. First, there was Jacques's death and losing Sophia. In her head, Zel always referred to Shelia's baby as Sophia. She never referred to her out loud, not even to Shelia.

They had spent the past five years coming to the place where they could have a conversation without the smog of Sophia choking words as they came out of their mouths. The fact that Zel stayed in Paris helped their relationship significantly. They could go weeks without speaking.

However, Zel would be back in Chicago in a couple of weeks. Their friendship was full of all the things that they didn't dare mention. Actually, there were just two things that they didn't mention—Sophia and Jacques.

Zel needed Shelia to be a real friend; she knew Shelia could do it. It was time for Shelia to hold up her end of the bargain. Memories flowed like ghosts in between every interaction, haunting Zel to this day.

Like the day she came back to the flat and found that Shelia had given birth and the baby was gone.

1997

Mama T had them house-sitting. It has one bedroom, but space enough for Sophia's bassinet. Shelia and Zel usually took turns sleeping between the bedroom and the dining room, which had a daybed instead of a table. They didn't have much money, and their place was pretty big considering. Plus, Zel was out of town at least one week a month so it was easier to manage.

It was weeks before the due date. Zel had taken a modeling job in Italy. She was only gone for a week. It was no time at all, but all the time in the world. Zel came back to Shelia lying on the bed with her back to the door, looking out of the window.

"Hey, Lia, baby, I'm home. How is my girl doing?" Zel started gushing, "I found the cutest outfits in Italy, but I know we can't afford a whole bunch of stuff, so I limited myself to only two of the cutest outfits. I figure I have to start designing for her myself. My little niece deserves couture."

Shelia rolled over. "Zel, listen."

Zel looked at Shelia's face. Mama T used the expression "death warmed over." Zel saw it now. There wasn't any spark in Shelia's eyes. Her face muscles stopped working, and the skin merely dropped from her face. The bags under her eyes were heavy and pronounced.

"Baby, are you OK? Do I need to call the doctor?"

"Listen, Zel. I had to do it. I had no other choice."

Zel slowly sat down on the bed and shook her head. "Do what? What are you talking about? Lia, what did you do?"

"I couldn't keep her."

Zel's mind raced. Couldn't keep her? Couldn't keep her? "No, no. We're going to raise her together. We have the bassinet. The whole house is ready. What do you mean you couldn't keep her? What did you do to her?" Zel looked in the bassinet. She whipped around the corner to the bathroom, and then came back in the bedroom. She shook Shelia. "Where is she?"

"I put her up for adoption. I couldn't keep her. She deserves a chance at a great life. The couple ... they know love. They would know how to love her. I had to do it. We couldn't keep her. She deserves the best. They can give that to her. She deserves that."

"We could have given her that. What are you talking about?"

"Rick doesn't even know about her. Mother doesn't know about her. You've transitioned energy about Jacques to her. She deserves a fresh start without our demons tugging at her ankles."

"You didn't. You couldn't. One week. I've been gone one week. When did you have the time?"

"Well, it does take longer than a week."

Then Zel got it. She knew all along. She let Zel buy clothes and get excited. She was planning on giving the baby up for adoption. Zel closed her eyes and saw black. She launched herself at Shelia's throat.

It wasn't until Shelia's slaps started penetrating her consciousness that she loosened her grip. Shelia rolled over, choking. Zel grabbed a jacket from the closet and left the suffocating apartment. Sitting on the step in front of the flat, Zel pulled out a cigarette. She stared at her shaking hands. She pursed her lips as tears streamed down her face.

God, she needed a drink, a smoke; hell, she needed something. What she needed was a little girl with Shelia's eyes and Rick's nose, or Shelia's hair and Rick's skinny legs. She had pictured her a thousand times, a thousand different ways, and had already loved her as if she belonged to Zel as well; but she hadn't belonged to Zel. Nothing belonged to Zel. She had a pretty face, a killer smile, a career, but she had longed for something to fill this empty hole in her heart.

Jacques had been gone now for six months, six months. Sometimes she still stopped on that street corner and sat on the ground. People looked at her like she was crazy. Even the tolerant Parisians looked at the sad girl who was sitting on a corner rocking and crying. It's amazing how people who are in your life for such a short time could mean so much. Jacques, Shelia's baby. Now she was rocking again.

The problem was that Zel knew that as bad as she felt, Shelia had to feel one hundred times worse, one thousand times worse. Shelia always did have trust issues. She gave Rick her all, but she didn't trust him. If she had trusted him, she would have told him. If she had believed in their love, she wouldn't have left. Zel truly believed that Shelia's trip to Paris had been her turning point. She had left Mother high and dry. Mama T told Zel during their frequent conversations that Mother had actually brought the police to her house saying she had stolen her child.

Of course, once the police found out that her child was older than eighteen and had left a note that she was leaving for Paris, they told her there was nothing they could do. Mother wasn't having any of that. She basically harassed Mama T.

Mama T had told her, "I've never seen that look in someone's eyes before. I understand the fear. If you had pulled this type of shit, I'd be in Paris looking for you, ready to beat your ass with what I could find. It's the pure hatred. She actually told me, 'You probably told Shelia to leave with Zel. You probably bought her ticket. You just wanted to ruin our family.' Zel, that's just crazy. I don't care enough about that woman to want to ruin her family."

Apparently, the ensuing articles sealed the deal. Mama T had promised not to tell Shelia's Mother anything. Zel knew if Mama T felt that it would be the right thing to do, she would have sung like a bird. Mother's crazy-ass attitude was her undoing. Once Mama T labeled you as crazy, she wouldn't help you across the street if you have one hand on a cane and the other clutching a million dollar check.

Zel knew, but Mother didn't. Mother never did quite think straight when it came to Shelia. Zel was starting to agree with Mother. Shelia deserved to have her ass whipped for the shit she was pulling.

Rick. Rick could stop her, but this situation … Zel couldn't call Rick. Not now. Before, when they first came to Paris, when she first found out, she could have called Rick; still, she wanted that baby so badly. She didn't want to share that baby, not even with its father.

She was going to be the one the baby was so excited to see when she walked through the door. The baby had been the light at the end of her very long, dark tunnel. And now the baby was gone. The light was gone. Hell, Zel would have adopted her herself had she known Shelia had no intention of raising the baby.

Zel let out a slow breath. Since that didn't work, she let out another. Since that didn't work, she started walking anywhere, everywhere, to the corner. She sat down and began to rock and hum under her breath. Mourning the man she loved who died, and the baby she loved who lived. Both lost to her by circumstances out of her control. The lights of her life extinguished.

Maybe she could have her own baby. She never had a problem finding a man. That's what she would do. She would have her own baby that no one could take away from her. She would nurture the baby in her body and watch it grow. She would take care of it after it was born. She could do it.

But now, right now, her body was her bread and butter. How would she care for a child if not with modeling? She would have to get a job. She could find work in the business. Hell, Mama T would support her, but she wouldn't be … Zel's eyes got really wide.

So that's what Shelia had been thinking. Her options had been even more limited than Zel's; but like Zel, she was not alone. However, she refused to share her burden. Until she learned she had people she could lean on, Zel didn't know how she was going make it. This world was too rough for alone.

Zel got up. Her sadness started turning into anger. Damn, Shelia. She knew from the beginning. She knew. She had allowed Zel to think, to dream, to prepare. She had allowed Zel to use her baby as a crutch and then pulled the crutch out from under her. She didn't even have the balls to tell Zel, "Look, don't worry about that corner of a room. The baby's never going to see it anyway."

Instead, the bitch had smiled and laughed and talked about what it would be like with the three of them. That baby had been hers, too; but the baby should have been Rick's. If Zel hadn't been so damn selfish and trusting—fuck.

If Zel had done what she should have done, called Rick and let him know the situation, it wouldn't have, couldn't have gotten this far.

Rick would have come. Now he was doing his basketball thing. Now his daughter was gone. Son of a bitch. No, daughter of a bitch. Bitch, bitch, bitch, bitch, bitch. The anger was boiling up in Zel right now.

Zel gave up walking and started to run. She ran until her lungs were bursting and her physical exhaustion matched her mental exhaustion, and she joined Shelia back at the flat for a depressed sleep. No talking. Just sleep.

The odd thing about it was, although Zel was doing well before Shelia gave birth, after the baby's birth her career took off. She was working with a photographer for some artistic shots. He was trying to get a range of emotions depending on the outfit she was wearing. He got to one that he said she needed to indicate sadness.

They tried everything, but he still wasn't getting the shot that he wanted. Finally, he snapped at her. "Surely, surely your life hasn't been all sunshine. No one's life has. You'll never get any further than pretty pictures if you can't connect with emotions. A dog that died. A cat that ran away." The tirade didn't work. Zel became more and more stiff.

Then the photographer stopped, stepped over to her, and sat her on a stool in the center of the room. He looked her in the eyes and told her to think of the most painful memory she could. The baby took hold of her mind. Her hand began to shake. He held her, kissed her on the top of her head, and said, "Let it go." He captured that first look of frailty and excruciating pain.

When she tried to wipe away the tears, he snapped at her. So with tears rolling down her face, on a stool with minimal light, she gave him what he wanted. Of all the beauty and high fashion shots she'd taken, it was still the one taken at the lowest point in her life that had shown up everywhere in Paris. The photo became legendary and Zel, the star, was born—the loneliest star in the constellation.

Shelia

2003

At any moment now Rick was going to answer her summons and meet her in a restaurant in town. No major news. She was a nobody, a nobody that didn't have the stomach to sit down at the table to wait for him. Instead, she was hiding out in the bathroom, pacing. What a piece of work she was, hiding out until a few minutes after their designated meeting time.

Women were looking at her like she had temporarily lost her mind. Her usual smile and nod of acknowledgement turned into a scary snarl. One lady had asked if there was something she could do to help. Unless she was prepared to turn back the clock or blink her out of here, there wasn't a thing to do. There wasn't anything that anyone could do except her.

Shelia had already splashed water on her face, ending up wetting her blouse and having to use the hand dryer to dry the spots.

Then of course, she ended up having to repair her make up. Now she was trying the relaxation exercises from her yoga video. They weren't working either. So she straightened her shoulders and walked as gracefully as she could back to her table.

He was there, waiting. He looked even better than he did at the party. Matter of fact, he looked better there than he did on television; and there she got more of the view with the tank and the shorts. On television, he was ripcord lean with muscles perfected as if Rodin personally had sculpted them.

Shelia had been to the Rodin museum in Paris. Granted the building, which was Rodin's house, needed a complete overhaul. The effort to keep the original house intact led to a floor patch job that was a bit scary to someone waddling with an extra human in tow. However, Rodin's style called to her. Similar to the way Rick's did. She didn't watch his games often. She had learned it was best if she didn't.

One time she had seen a glimpse of his eight pack on the court. Shelia had almost attacked Devon that night. She surprised them both because she never took the initiative. Devon was up for the challenge. That night, they soaked the mattress with their sweat. There were so many wet spots, they couldn't figure out if it was her, him, or the sweat they produced. They had to flip the mattress to get any sleep.

Rick looked up as she walked toward him, and she stopped in the middle of the restaurant. There was something about Rick that brought instant heat. She should have known better than to think she could go from a complete chicken to Superwoman in one day. Shelia turned to head back to the bathroom, but he caught up with her.

"Do you have a bladder control issue? Do you need a doctor or something? 'Cuz you kill every bathroom at every place we're at."

"No, no, I'm coming to the table now."

"Oh. It looked as if panic set in and you were going back to the bathroom."

"Yeah. Panic would be one way to describe it."

"Can we sit down before the scene becomes any bigger?"

Shelia let Rick lead her back to her seat.

"Wow, it's really good to see you. I had no idea until this moment how much I've missed you."

"Well, you're the one that packed your shit and left without so much as a goodbye. I had to hear the sorry-ass excuse from Mama T. Then when you decided to come back, you got married right away. Now, you've hidden in the bathroom twice, rather than have a conversation. That sounds like someone who was pining for me."

Shelia's eyes grew round with shock. Hmm. This was a bit different than she expected. They weren't friends anymore. She knew that. Everything that happened would forever prevent that, but he had unleashed his verbal pimp hand. His words came from nowhere and slapped the shit out of her, leaving her stunned.

Rick looked fierce as he said, "Did you think I was coming here for a reunion? A reunion with a married woman? For some sentimental bullshit like that? I came for answers. Zel wouldn't give them. I've been wondering for years what the hell happened. So figure out what you want to eat, and tell me what the hell happened to you all those years ago!"

"Wait. You talked to Zel?"

"Of course, she and Mama T keep me looking fly off the court. What rock have you been under? Mama T made my draft suit. I've been going back to her ever since."

"Zel didn't tell me you were that close."

"Yeah well, that's between the two of you. I've wanted to know for years what happened that summer."

"Jacques died."

"OK. I get that. I get why you and Zel flew to Paris. What I don't get is why you broke up with me before you left or why you stayed."

Shelia looked him in the eye. She should have been prepared for that question. It would have been the first question that she would have asked in the same position. Why she didn't recognize that he would want to know the same thing was a mystery. She had just called the number and asked him to an early dinner. That was all she did. She didn't know what to expect. He seemed so refined, so beyond her, beyond them.

Now, his eyes were blazing and his hands were shaking. She looked at his contorted face. She could see that a wrong word from her and the verbal slaps would be the last of her worries.

Mama T had told them once, "Listen, a man should never hit a woman. It's wrong. It's inexcusable. If it gets to that point, the two of you are over. However, that does not give you a free ride; because at the same time, there are certain things you can say to a man or do to a man, after which, I suggest you duck and run."

Shelia was sure as she was sitting there, that had she revealed to Rick that she was pregnant when she left, didn't tell him and gave his child up for adoption, she'd be one ducking heifer.

"I guess I was scared. Everything had happened so fast with us. I met you. I fell in love. I didn't know how to handle it. Zel needed me. I left."

"That simple, huh? That easy. Fuck Rick. Fuck me. One minute we're down, the next thing I knew you were gone, because you were 'scared.' I didn't matter at all. My feelings didn't matter at all. Fuck Rick. He'll be alright. Right. Fuck the nigga' that loved you. Right? Hey, fuck that nigga'. One minute I'm in a relationship. The next minute I'm reading your letter. A letter. You didn't have the fuckin' balls to tell me to my face."

"I didn't have the courage. How do you break up with the man you love?"

"That wasn't love. Are you kidding me? Couldn't have been. If it was love, you would have stayed."

"But Zel—"

Rick held up his hand and shook his head. "You would have stayed. Listen, this is ... I can't. I have better things to do." Rick got up and threw a few bills on the table.

Shelia nodded, closed her eyes, and looked down as he walked away. She gathered her things, wrapped her arms around her middle and hustled out of the restaurant.

She hadn't expected Rick to spew bitterness at her and definitely not at ninety miles an hour. She might admit that she deserved it, but she hadn't expected it. This Rick was different from the man she loved in college. He was always smiling on television and in his interviews. He seemed so happy and well-adjusted. Surely, a brief relationship with her all those years ago … she couldn't do it. She couldn't say that it couldn't have meant much to him, since it had meant the world to her.

As she drove home, she started crying uncontrollably. Her breath hitched every time she inhaled. She just wanted to go home. Half an hour later, she pulled into her driveway and pushed the button on top of the visor. She jabbed at it, and her garage door didn't respond. She slammed the gear into park, and gave in to her tears.

AYAAN

2003

"*Mommy,* look, the neighbor lady is in our driveway crying?"

Ayaan and Kendall had come out in the front yard for a few minutes after dinner to chase fireflies. Kendall had her jar, and she'd run around on the grass. She never did catch a firefly. She just liked to run around. Ayaan liked watching her laughing and running in circles. Every once in a while, Kendall would say, "See mommy. See. There's one." Then she'd giggle and run around some more.

Today, though, they were both staring at Shelia, who had taken it upon herself to park in the driveway and start crying. Ayaan rolled her eyes. Incredible. Really? What the hell was she supposed to do now? Ayaan stood with her hands on her hips, but obviously Shelia didn't notice.

Kendall started running towards the car.

"Stop."

Kendall stopped in her tracks and looked back.

"What did I tell you about going up to strangers?"

"She's not a stranger. She's the neighbor lady."

"What's her name?"

Kendall let out an exasperated sigh. "I don't know. I forgot to ask when I invited her to my party." Kendall tilted her head and smiled. "I can ask her now."

Ayaan smiled back. "Or you can go back inside and have Cleo run your bathwater."

"But you always run my bathwater."

"Go inside, Kendall."

"But what if she needs me?"

Ayaan's breath hitched. The innocent questions from her daughter got to the root of the problem. What if Shelia decided she needed Kendall? Ayaan balled her hands, digging her nails into her palm. She clenched her jaw. "Kendall, come give your mother a hug."

Kendall, acknowledging defeat, trudged over to Ayaan and gave her a hug. "If you need me, I'll be upstairs."

"Thanks, that's very sweet of you. Now skedaddle youngun'." Ayaan playfully swatted Kendall on her rear.

Kendall laughed, got out of reach, and shook her rear. Then, she ran into the house calling for Cleo.

Ayaan looked at the car. Shelia hadn't budged. What the hell? Ayaan wanted to go back in the house and leave Shelia right where she was. If the bitch wanted to bawl in her driveway, fuck it. Let her. The heifer shouldn't be out here anyway.

Ayaan resolutely walked to her door. She turned around one last time. "Dammit," stamped her foot and then stalked toward the car. She rapped on the window hurting her fingers. That just pissed her off more.

Shelia raised her face, sniffling. She turned on the car battery and rolled down the window.

"Is there any reason you're in my driveway?"

Shelia looked around and gave a self-deprecating laugh. "That would explain why my garage door opener didn't work. I'm so sorry." Shelia turned the car all the way on.

Ayaan rolled her eyes. "Open the door."

"No, I'm sorry. I'll just go home now."

"Open it."

Shelia turned off the engine.

Ayaan climbed into the passenger seat. They sat in quiet for a while.

"Listen, I really did mean to go home."

"Yeah, but instead you're here. You have got to be the 'cryingest' person on the face of the earth. What happened now?"

Shelia paused and then shrugged. "I don't know. The ozone layer is deteriorated. I just kind of got choked up all of a sudden. What we gonna' do?"

Betrayed by Shelia's unexpected sense of humor, Ayaan snorted. Then she gathered herself enough to glare at Shelia.

Shelia thinned out her lips, broke eye contact first, and looked down at her hands.

"What do you want?"

Shelia started the car. "I really should go home."

"I asked you a question."

"Yes. Yes, you did. I'm sorry I disturbed you."

"This can't go on."

Shelia had the good sense not to respond or pretend that she didn't know what Ayaan meant.

Ayaan got out of the car and watched as Shelia navigated over to her house. She walked into the house to give Cleo back her evening. Bedtime was her job. There was no way that Kendall would happily go down without Ayaan reading her a story. Ayaan had work to do. She didn't have time to let Shelia live all up in her mind.

Kendall had all sorts of questions about the sad neighbor lady.

Ayaan didn't have any good answers. Finally, Ayaan had to explain that sometimes even grown-ups didn't know what other grown-ups were thinking. Ayaan could only hope that Shelia would get help. With that, she kissed Kendall on the forehead and eased herself out of the room. She then hustled to the kitchen for a well-deserved glass of wine.

She could hear Kendall humming to herself and singing songs. The minute Kendall could talk she started mimicking the songs on the radio. It might not seem like much, but truth be told, it's an eye-opening experience to hear your daughter singing about someone paying her bills. Next thing, she was going to shake it fast. So now, Radio Disney was their best friend. Thank goodness for Disney sanitizing every single lyric.

The wine went down really smoothly. Ayaan wasn't much of a wine connoisseur. She just liked what she liked. This particular sweet red would go to her head pretty fast. Even now, though, she couldn't get wasted. She was the mother of a five-year-old daughter.

And that girl was bright as hell. This was one relationship that she had to get right. She couldn't mess this up like she did her marriage. OK. She didn't mess it up per se. Marriage is a two-way street.

The problem with starting out as friends with Kenneth, was that she made assumptions. They both made assumptions. They knew so much about each other that they thought they knew everything. Ayaan realized you could never know everything about a person. You could be handcuffed to someone for ten years, and on day two of the tenth year you'd learn something you couldn't have guessed in a million years.

1997

The minute Ayaan and Kenneth were married, Ayaan started talking about having children. It was natural for her. They were married, in love, and making good money. They would love a baby so well. She had enough saved for a surrogate, and she was ready to go. However, Kenneth was a bit more hesitant.

"Kenneth, I don't understand. This way we can have a baby who is our baby. People do it all the time."

"I'm not sure about it. That's all. I need to do a bit more investigating."

"Babe, all you have to do is jag off into a cup. Leave the rest to me."

Kenneth rubbed his hand over his face. "I can't just leave the rest to you. This is a baby. This is our baby." He picked up her hands. "We should be in this together. I'm just asking for time."

She ignored his request and started looking for a baby to adopt. Kenneth used to joke that he had yet to get this kind of determination at the office. She covered all of her bases. Unless Kenneth was needed on some documentation, she kept him out of the process.

He assumed they had years. It turned out they had months. Ayaan guessed that was why he was so shocked when she came to him with a letter from one of their adoption lawyers. This one had a colleague in France.

Ayaan had walked into the office, waving the letter. "Tell me I'm brilliant."

Kenneth laughed. They both knew that Ayaan was smart and creative. When she called herself brilliant, she had really pulled a rabbit out of the hat.

He leaned back in his chair, playing with his pencil. "I guess you're alright. I mean I don't have any complaints, but I can give you a few suggestions. Shall we start with the kitchen and work our way up? Or down depending on your mood?"

Ayaan walked around the desk and sat in his lap. "For this, you will eat every dry piece of meat that I put in front of you and swear it is steak from Morton's. That's how good your wife is. It's amazing that you ended up with me. As brilliant as I am, I should have held out for a Kennedy."

"Are you kidding me? I'm the one that should have held out for a nice older lady who would have wanted to spoil me with money."

Ayaan laughed and kissed him on the neck. Then she bit him on the ear.

"Ow. I didn't do anything when you were ready to toss me aside for a Kennedy."

"Hell, that's your problem, you spoiled brat."

"OK, what happened? Why is my wife brilliant now?"

"OK, so you know we've been looking to adopt?"

2003

Ayaan took another sip of her wine.

Back then, she should have felt the change in the air. She should have sensed his stillness. There had to have been some sign that she missed in all her excitement. She was so excited that she was literally bouncing on his lap. That's when he asked her to take a seat. She didn't realize until months later that it was that instant that she had begun losing him.

"Sweetie, you're killing my lap. Why don't you sit over there?"

He had never said those words. He had never pushed her away before. She was so wrapped up in getting everything she'd ever wanted that she hadn't paid attention. She moved to the seat and started babbling about Paris. It had taken a long time before she brought the end of her marriage back to that moment. To realize one dream, she had to give up on another. She made that sacrifice. She did it. She didn't even think about it. She never hesitated. She walked away.

His guilt was enormous. That's why she was still an equal partner, even though she didn't do any work. It wasn't enough for her. Their company made enough money to support her and Kendall, easily, but she had something to prove. She didn't need him or his money.

However, late at night with a glass of wine and silence plucking gaps in the carefully constructed shield around her heart, she knew that she yearned to end the evening with him across from her with his own glass of wine sharing their day's experiences. She ached to watch him cooking in the kitchen and walk up to him and wrap her arms around his waist, as they rocked to music only they could hear. She craved his scent on the pillow next to hers. She longed to laugh at jokes that only two people who grew up as straight nerds could appreciate.

Yeah, she missed him.

She missed who she was with him. She rarely dedicated this kind of time to thinking about what she didn't have. What she did have was so amazing that sometimes she felt guilty for wanting more. She felt ungrateful for wanting it all. Although it was true, she didn't need him at all, still she wanted him so badly.

Zel

2003

Zel stood in front of Rodin's sculpture. Rodin's gardens always gave her peace and she needed a bit of peace now. She was a week away from her trip to the States, and she was a bit nervous. She had asked Shelia to come to her in Paris. She had asked her to drop everything and hang out with her. She knew Shelia was going to say, "No." She just hadn't said it yet. Zel could probably push, prod, and manipulate. It might work; but ultimately, she just wanted Shelia to come because she had asked.

She knew Shelia had Devon and all, but it really wasn't as if it was a match made in heaven. Who were they kidding? She couldn't even remember the last vacation they took together. It might actually have been their honeymoon, which was little more than a long weekend getaway.

Zel got a lot of her best ideas just clearing her mind and standing in front of the Thinking Man statue. He had the weight of the world on his shoulders, and he was just letting all his problems ramble around in his head until he found a solution. He had been thinking about his problems for decades. It sort of made her problems seem manageable.

Instead of staying in the house, Zel made her way to the gardens where she sat on a bench. She liked to think she was a bit of an artist in her own right. Her clothing designs were well received, but she couldn't imagine mimicking the perfect human body in metal. She was good. He was a genius. So here she was trying to soak in a bit of genius.

Zel took off her huge, sun-blocking hat and put it beside her on the bench. Surely, her skin could take five minutes of direct Parisian sunlight. It's not as if she was sitting on the equator. Her modeling career was declining anyway. It didn't take a genius to figure that out. That's why she was concentrating more on her clothing line, as well as a few other business ventures.

She had even tried her hand at the first relationship that counted since Jacques. Six months into it, she realized that he wasn't the man for her. The sad part was that he loved her. It was real, honest, and the kind that she had thought she was waiting for. His love was seductive. She felt cherished. The problem was she also felt restless and bored.

He was content with just her. Everything was nice. He worked at a nice office job. He looked nice. He was nice. He treated her nice. They had nice, intelligent conversations. They had nice dinners. They went to nice restaurants. They made nice love. She had nice fake orgasms. And that was that.

Everyone loved him. What was there not to love? Or maybe love was the wrong word. No one was opposed to him. Zel just wasn't invested in the relationship. That was the crux of the problem. She could really use a best friend to help her figure out what to do, but she didn't have Shelia. She had Rodin. Rodin never offered advice. He offered peace.

As she looked at the statue, she let her mind wander. She had met Paul on Jacques's corner. She still went there every now and again to gain perspective, torture herself, whatever. Well actually, when she was lonely she went there. At least she didn't break down now into a blubbering mess. She considered that progress. She would just pop a squat for about five to ten minutes. Usually, people left her alone. It wasn't as if she had a cup for coins in front of her.

Nice guys don't let women sit on the curb alone. They ask if you need help. When you say no, they inquire why you are sitting on the ground. They ask you for coffee. They share their sad story. They ask if they can call you. They take you to nice shows. Next thing you know, you're kissing the nice guy, because even nice guys eventually make a move. You kiss him back because it doesn't cost you anything. Then, you're in the nice guy relationship.

The simple thing would be to break up with the nice guy. The problem was he was the nice guy. She didn't want to break the nice guy's heart. However, just like the nice guy eventually made a move, the nice guy also tried to take the relationship to the next level. Zel already went to the sex level to her dire disappointment.

Paul was originally from North Carolina, but they were in France. Fake orgasms shouldn't be needed in France. The very thought of it seemed so un-French. There should be passion coming out of the ass. There should be footsie-playing under the table. There should be hot, dark, dangerous looks. There should be kisses that end with him pulling her down on the bed by her hair.

Zel blew out a hard breath. Now she was wet—and this was how she had to get wet. She either thought about someone else or she thought about what they could be doing, not what they were doing. What they *were* doing was putting her to sleep. Sometimes she would see a guy walking down the street. He'd be fine and black, white, Latino, Asian, it didn't matter anymore. She didn't have a type. She just needed him to know how to work it. The images she'd have of what they could be doing were vivid. Sometimes she pulled them up when she was with Paul.

136

To be honest, it wasn't just the fact that he was nice. He listened to her. She told him about Jacques and Sophia. She laid her head on his shoulder and cried. He held her. That was the kind of caring one couldn't buy, and she hadn't gotten it from the men she had dated since Jacques. She knew Paul cared in a way that others hadn't. Maybe that was the seductive part. It was possible that was the part that allowed an average kiss to lead to more. He took care of her heart.

The guilt, though, was beginning to eat away at her. He deserved the best. Without a doubt, he deserved a woman who would stand still with him and enjoy the silences. He helped to heal her. He helped her realize that she needed to see Shelia and really talk to her. They needed to clear the air. Shelia was always running from conversations about Sophia and Rick.

Zel wasn't helping that situation. She knew Rick was a client at Devon's firm. Out of all the law firms in Chicago, the fact that he had ended up at "Schmuck for Hire" astounded her. She also knew he was going to that anniversary celebration. To have told Shelia would have given her time to make excuses and run like the wind. The time for running was over. Shelia had said, herself, that she was going to start dealing with things. It seemed fitting that she should start with Rick. Why not?

The funny thing is that lately Shelia must really be falling apart. Mother called Zel to thank her for an outfit from her collection. She'd just casually mentioned how she might need to take in Shelia's dress because she had lost so much weight over the last month. That was major for Mother. Normally, Mother just wrote thank you notes. She never called Zel, unless it was to make a request. Shit, if she was that pissed off about an unapproved year in Paris, she'd stroke out over an unplanned pregnancy, illegitimate child, and adoption.

That's really why Zel was going back. It was time to lay a lot to rest. For Zel, it was clearly time to lay Jacques and Sophia to rest. To do that properly, she was going to have to talk to Shelia about that time. The taboo subjects—the ones that always had Shelia changing the conversation, hanging-up the phone, and now apparently running to public bathrooms to hide.

Zel tossed back her head and laughed. The fact that Shelia kept running to the bathroom tickled Zel more than a little bit, and Rick was so pissed when he called Zel to tell her about their lunch or lack thereof, he was livid. He went off for about fifteen minutes. Zel let the rant continue until he paused for a breath.

He admitted that he thought whatever they had was done. It was over. However, sitting across from her … he completely lost his cool. He thought he was unflappable. However, seeing her at the celebration dinner was a shock. He thought he had handled it well. Obviously, he had years of pain built up and it exploded all over the place.

Then he realized what Shelia had not yet—Zel had known they both were going to be at the party.

"Here's the thing, Rick. I've always said that what is or is not between you has nothing to do with me. So I figured I'd just let it ride and see what happened. It got you two talking."

"No, it got her hiding in the bathroom and me trying not to strangle her in a restaurant. I don't consider that good times."

"But you didn't strangle her. I call that progress."

"That's because you're crazy. I'll holla' at you later."

She hadn't spoken with him since. Mama T had at least heard from him. He was still breathing and dressing fly. Her friendship, if that's what you could call her relationship with Rick, was built on too big a secret for her to ever really consider them close friends. Their house of cards had been leaning precariously for a while. Rick was cool as hell. He's one of those people who had that charisma that pulled people in. It wasn't built on arrogance.

One time last year, he had come to Paris to hang out with Zel and convinced her to go to the gym. Zel, who ran to help manage her weight, agreed. What she hadn't counted on was weight training. All of a sudden, her puny muscles were doing their best to lift reps, and they weren't happy about it.

2002

It was almost like he got a kick out of torturing her at the gym. The more she strained and sweated, the happier he seemed to get. He was singing to his tunes and dancing as he encouraged, "Three more." The good thing about Rick was at least he could shake it well. The bad thing was when you're straining to finish fifteen reps, your muscles are screaming, and your companion is dancing, you want to revert back to kicking people in the ankles.

The looks she gave him usually sent people scurrying to the corners. He merely laughed and continued dancing. He was hopping to the next machine, while she was dragging until he clearly had worked all the nice out of her body and she gave up. "My body doesn't do that."

"You can push your body beyond what your mind is telling you that you can't do."

"Listen, punk ass, I'm done. You take your NBA eight pack and kick bricks. You can call me again when you want to do something like go to a show, go to a restaurant, walk along the Seine, anything but workout."

Rick raised one eyebrow and asked, "Anything?"

"Eww. Anything suitable for siblings is suitable for us."

Rick laughed. "That leaves out a lot of good stuff. Sure you don't want to be kissing cousins?"

Zel stuck out her tongue.

He put his arm around her shoulder. "You know I never had a sister before. This could be fun. Are you my older sister? Do you pay when we go out?"

"Really? I'm too tired for this shit and for those comments, you are buying me dinner." Zel brushed past Rick and stalked into the locker room. Though she knew he wasn't serious about the light flirting he was doing, she still thought Shelia was crack-head crazy for breaking up with him.

After Rick took her to dinner, Zel decided she needed to speak with Shelia. She really needed to come to Paris. This was ridiculous. How was she supposed to lay her ghosts to rest if she never confronted them?

It was about noon for Shelia. So Zel gave her a call.

She immediately answered.

Zel started in. "OK. You don't have to move here, but you can come for a visit."

Shelia laughed. "Do you really want me to stop answering your phone calls?"

"I'm serious. It will be good for you."

"Why do you continue to push for me to move back to Paris?"

"You were happy here."

Shelia got really quiet for a moment before she said, "Yeah, at one time I was. That time was forever ago. It surely didn't end that way."

"You were happier than you are now."

"Hmm. Tell me about your latest show. When am I getting my dress? I live for your creations."

It was Zel's turn to get quite. The old subject switch again. Shelia wasn't even subtle. She just stopped talking about whatever and asked a question. When it came to Sophia or their time in Paris, it was always going to be a very short conversation.

Zel didn't know how to break through the barrier. So she just started talking. "I know you don't want to talk about Paris. You want to pretend it was a lifetime ago. You want to pretend it never happened. It did happen. She existed. For a short time, you were someone's mother."

Shelia's breath caught. "Don't do this, Zel."

"No. Wait. It's not what you think. I'm not saying it to be hurtful. I'm saying that you never talk about it. You never talk about her. I'm the only one in this world who knows she exists. Well, I'm the only one in your world who knows she exists. And we don't talk about her. Ever. You always change the subject."

Zel heard Shelia's breathing on the other end of the line.

"Shelia, I miss her. You have to miss her, too. Whatever she was to me, she was so much more to you, and I want to be there for you. I know you haven't forgotten. You can't avoid it forever. You have to deal with it."

"Why do I have to deal with it, Zel? She has a new life. I have a new life. Matter of fact, Devon wants to have children."

"Yeah, you've been singing that tune since you were married. He's been waiting children for three-plus years. Has the stick turned blue yet?"

Silence.

"You have no intention of having that man's baby. We both know that."

"You don't know anything, Zel."

"I know that every time I see you there is a tinge of sadness in your eyes. I know that I haven't seen you laugh so hard that you cry in years."

"Maybe, Zel, you've stopped being funny."

"Could be or maybe you carry her around in your heart like a fucking anvil."

"You seem to be the only one complaining. Devon isn't. How is your man doing? Wait. Do you have a man, or are you still pining for the one that's six feet under?"

"Too much, Shelia."

"Oh, we can talk about my pain. We can be all open and honest about my shit. We can run down the issues that I've had in my life, but the minute we mention the fact that you can't move beyond a three-month affair, it's too far. Well, too damn bad. You need to get back on the horse and ride it till it screams, or did you go from being a model to a nun without telling me?"

"Too far."

"Not far enough. You're all up in and around mine. What about you? Why don't you get out the rusty key to your chastity belt, dust off your twat, and get some? Why not? Paris is the City of Love."

"I will, if you will. You come to Paris and honestly deal with your feelings about Sophia, and I will get the dust off my twat."

"Why is it so damn important for me to come to Paris? Paris doesn't hold good memories for me. Shit. I don't know why you stayed. It shouldn't provide good memories for your ass either. You should have packed up shop a long time ago. Dead people don't come back."

"Why didn't you just have an abortion, since dead people don't come back? You wouldn't have to torture yourself over the existence of your baby. You could have had her sucked out with a vacuum and gone on about your business."

"You bitch. You have no clue about the decision that I had to make."

"You had to make. You had to make? Really? Were you being abused? No. Was he an addict? Nope. No, you had a great guy and a bitch-ass attitude without a spine. You didn't have to send your baby away. You *chose* to send your baby away. There is a difference."

"You didn't have to keep your body as a shrine to your dead boyfriend. You chose to. There is a difference. We all make choices in this life. At least, I took care of my baby. I didn't suck her out with a vacuum. I gave her to a couple that loves her."

"Her daddy loved her. Wait. My bad. Her daddy could have loved her. He didn't know, though, did he? Just because your dad left your ass didn't mean that her father was going to leave her."

"She's loved."

"How do you know? You handed her off and hoped for the best. You don't know shit about the couple. How much could you learn from one interview? Did you even get their last name?"

"The lawyer checked them out. So do you plan on being buried beside Jacques tomorrow, or are you going to wait another year or two?"

"Like you care. Do you plan on waiting for Sophia to grow up, look you up, and give you permission to have another kid; or are going to keep worshipping at the altar of the child you gave away?"

"Well, at least I haven't completely given up any semblance of a social life. I, at least, got married."

"You don't even love that man. You are living with little more than a complete workaholic stranger. You call that a marriage."

"It's more of a marriage than yours. Married to a dead man. Is your life being scripted by Tim Burton?"

"I'll take mine over yours any day."

"Well, I guess that's where we differ."

"I guess it is."

"For the record, I know my child is happy, because I know exactly where she is and who she's with, and it's not in Paris, bitch." With that, Shelia hung up the phone.

Zel stopped pacing and sat down on the couch. *Sonofabitch. Shelia won. Hands down. For real? God bless it. Shit and Damn. Wow. Really?* Zel couldn't move for a half an hour. She just kept the conversation going in her head. *She had a life. She had friends. She just didn't want empty promiscuous sex. So she didn't sleep around. Not sleeping around was supposed to be good. Not sleeping around was supposed to be great.*

At one point, Zel loved sex. She truly did love a good orgasm. *When was the last time I had one? Crap. I haven't had a good orgasm since a year after Jacques died.* She tried, but no one was making her cum. Since she wasn't cumming, she stopped worrying about sex and concentrated on her career. *Have I really been celibate for four years?*

It took Shelia to point it out. Zel's anger began to dissipate. Shelia never mentioned Jacques. He had always fallen in line with Sophia. Zel hadn't thought Shelia had an opinion. Apparently, she did and it was clearly not what Zel expected.

2003

At the time, Zel thought she was saving Shelia. That was not the case. After that argument, Zel thought about getting back on the dating bandwagon, but as the years passed, the quality of men had truly gone down. A few months ago, she started going out with Paul. It was like learning to walk before you can run again.

She still wanted Shelia to come to Paris. She might still need to lay Sophia to rest. Zel needed her, too. She held onto Jacques for so long that she couldn't figure out how to let him go again. That was the hardest part of all of this. She was stuck. She needed a change. So if the mountain wouldn't come to her, she would go to the mountain.

Maybe what she needed was the energy of Chicago to help her release Jacques. Even now, sitting in Rodin's garden, she felt his presence. At the corner, she felt his presence. She wanted Shelia to help her get past that.

Chicago didn't hold any memories of Jacques. Maybe it was better this way. She'd find out soon enough.

AYAAN

1997

As Ayaan prepared for the trip to Paris for the interview that she hoped would get her the child she so desperately wanted, it seemed as if yesterday she was walking toward Kenneth in her custom-made white dress. It was made by the same woman who made her high school prom dress.

For prom, she wanted something different than what the other girls were wearing. At the same time, her mother was very conservative. She couldn't wear anything that didn't reach the knees. She couldn't show cleavage. It couldn't be too revealing. She was a girl, and she refused to wear a potato sack. While her father went along with her mother's rules, he gave her room for interpretation. Her mother wouldn't budge. So he went with her to a dressmaker on North Lincoln Avenue for her prom dress.

It was a combination of two different dresses that covered her at top and cascaded on the bottom. It was "fly" even if Ayaan did say so herself.

Slowly over the years, Kenneth had replaced her friends. They had gotten married so much younger than she had. So when she was still kicking it, they were having play dates. When it was time for her to get married, they were there, but they weren't really engaged in the event. They went through book after book of wedding dresses, but nothing was unique enough. So she pulled some options together and went to the only seamstress she knew, the woman that her father trusted to make her prom dress. Since her parents were long gone, it made sense to go back to her.

The fact that she had to walk down the aisle by herself was hard enough. She thought her parents should have some role. So it was her father's seamstress and her mother's purse. Even though they had never met Kenneth, she knew that they would approve.

He was something special that she never thought she'd find. She figured that she was going to have to settle when it came to her mate. As much as she liked kicking it, she had gotten to the point that she wanted something secure.

The guys that she dated were lacking in one way or another. She saw a couple guys consistently. There was the guy she could talk to on the phone all night long, but the thought of having sex with him … well, she couldn't imagine it. There was the guy that cleaned her pipes on a regular basis. They fit in the bedroom so well that it was astonishing how little they had to talk about the minute the sun rose. Really astounding.

She had discussed them both with Kenneth at one time or another. He seemed to think that you couldn't have a relationship with someone you couldn't talk to. She was in the other camp. She'd rather be with the man cleaning her pipes. She always had Kenneth to talk to if she needed conversation. So why did she need it from her man?

But she was lucky enough to get both with Kenneth. That made the walk down the aisle even sweeter. She was a grown woman who had given her heart fully to the man at the other end of the aisle. Her steps were as sure as her heart. She knew this was it. In reality, she hadn't known shit.

It started with a small fracture, infinitesimal. So small she had completely missed it. They spent their honeymoon in Mexico. She had ended up getting stranded in the ocean, then due to salt water and alcohol that might have been mixed in with a little Montezuma's revenge, she also spent time praying to the porcelain god.

She had hoped that Kenneth would never see her like that. She had planned a tight body upkeep schedule, so he would never again see the wolf come out. That one time at the hospital was bad enough. She was convinced she was going to be the hot, cool wife that Kenneth's friends would envy.

However, in starting their marriage dry heaving over a foreign toilet, that strategy flew right out of the window. Even worse, the doctor had to come to the hotel room to give her a shot in the ass. That had to be sexy as hell.

However, this wasn't Mexico, this was Paris. Paris was sexy as hell. She went all out, buying a new suit for the interview and new undies for afterward. They planned on spending five days. It would be a quick trip, but they had managed to get some work done over there as well. They were going to do a consult with a Parisian. It even sounded cool.

The evenings, though, were for her and Kenneth. They were going to show the Parisians how it was done. While Kenneth was good for romance, she wanted to get some "burn the bed sheets" heat as well. She had spent the last week almost bouncing off the walls as they prepared for their trip.

Kenneth had been much more subdued, yet every time she asked him if he was OK, he said yes. He was just a bit stressed about leaving the company. He didn't know if they were going to be able to get Web connectivity in France. He was always worried about something, always with a crease in his forehead. They all sounded legitimate.

Ayaan kept shopping and packing and talking and hoping that the interview would go well.

The girl was nineteen and American. She was due in two months and realized that she couldn't keep the baby. She wanted her baby raised in the United States. She'd prefer it if she was raised close to Chicago. That's how Ayaan had gotten the call. She was sure there were other couples that fit the profile, but the girl said there was something about them that seemed right. Even though they were only one of three being interviewed, they'd have to convince her that they would be the best to raise her baby.

They were successful in their own way. They had savings that were more than enough to carry them, as they kept the site running and expanding. There was nothing stopping them. As Ayaan continued packing, she realized that it might be better to break out one of her outfits to get Kenneth in the mood before the flight. They were leaving directly after work, and the first forty-eight hours in Paris promised to be short on sleep.

Ayaan looked through her luggage and unpacked a delectable little number complete with a black bustier that gave her the good high cleavage. She added the matching garter and thigh-high fishnet stockings. She slipped her feet into red patent leather high heels and rushed to the kitchen to fix a quick plate of snacks to keep Kenneth's energy up. This was going to be a hell of a night before a hell of a week.

She heard Kenneth's key in the door as she finished slicing strawberries. She was pumped. She quickly hefted the plate in one hand and casually walked into the living room. "How's it going handsome?"

Kenneth looked her over from head to toe and then started at the head again. He walked over, removed the plate, and put in on the table. He walked back and grabbed her by the waist and pulled her close. He kissed her in a way they hadn't had time for since this Paris frenzy began. Then he did something really odd. He hugged her tight and held on for life.

At first, she thought he was overcome with need. Usually that meant rushing to the bedroom, couch, floor. It didn't include desperate hugs. And this hug was getting a bit desperate.

Ayaan pulled back. "What's going on?"

Kenneth took a deep breath. "We need to talk." He took her hand and walked her over to the couch. She had pulled out her best sneaky freaky, and that made him want to talk. Shit, this was bad.

Ayaan pulled her hand back. She held up a finger indicating that she needed a minute. She walked into the bedroom and changed into a pair of jogging pants and a T-shirt. If they were going to talk, she was damn sure going to be fully dressed.

She walked back into the living room, sat down beside Kenneth, and waited.

When he didn't say anything, she started. "Who is she?"

"Who?"

"The bitch I'm going to have to cut as soon as I slice your balls in half."

Kenneth smiled. "You made your position on cheating very clear. There isn't anyone else. For one, I'm not crazy; and for two, I love you."

"What are we talking about then?"

The smile left Kenneth's face. "Let's not go. Let's not go to Paris."

Ayaan was confused. "Are you worried about the flight? You've taken an airplane before. It'll be longer than Mexico, but it will be all right."

Kenneth took Ayaan's hands into his. "Listen, I know you really want a child. I get it; but I didn't … I don't …. I never saw myself as a father."

Ayaan just looked at Kenneth.

"I love you, and I love our life. I love everything that we have.

And I'm excited about us and the company. I just don't seem to be as excited as you are about adding a child."

"I don't understand. You knew we were looking into adoption."

Kenneth jumped up. "I know. I get it, but I thought we had time. I thought we were just going to look into it. I didn't know that we were suddenly going to start interviewing prospective birth mothers in another country. How would I have guessed that? How?"

Ayaan tilted her head and pursed her lips. "What did you think I was doing? I want to be a mother, you know that."

"I'm not sure I want to be a father."

"We're supposed to leave tomorrow night. They're expecting us."

Kenneth sat back down and took Ayaan's hands. "Please understand. I need more time. This is a big adjustment that I can't get my head around."

Ayaan snorted. "That's why you married me, isn't it? My plumbing didn't work. I was perfect for you. What? Did you think just because I had to get my insides yanked out that I got my heart yanked out at the same time? Do you think just because I can't carry a child that the desire for a child would disappear, too? Is that what you thought?" Ayaan began yanking at her hands.

Kenneth held on a bit tighter.

"Let. Me. Go."

Kenneth let go of her hands, and she walked to the other side of the living room and looked out over their view of Lake Michigan. If she adjusted her perception, she could also see their living room mirrored behind her. It wasn't big, but it was beautiful. The cream leather furniture looked exquisite on top of the cream carpet. The glass coffee table sat between the couch and two Lazy Boy chairs. Kenneth was still on the couch looking at her. She adjusted her perception again so that she was looking out over Lake Michigan.

"Ayaan, I married you because I love you. You have to know that. You have to feel that. You have to know deep within you. I made a fool of myself for you. I would call you for no apparent reason. Do you really think that I wanted to be friends with a female? Please. That friendship was an investment. I just wanted you around me until I could figure out a way to reel you in."

"Please, Kenneth. You know as well as I do that you were picking up women right and left."

"Yes, I was picking up women right and left. I tried to pick you up, remember? Our first date was supposed to be the two of us eating breakfast. You invited one of your girlfriends. Who does that? Who invites a friend to a date? It wasn't as if it was at my house. It was at a restaurant. We were meeting there."

"We've been over this."

"Yes, we have, but I need you to understand. I was your friend because I wanted to be more, but you were dealing with those dusty, goofy-ass men."

"Yeah, but those dusty, goofy-ass men were men enough to want to raise a child."

Kenneth got up and sat on the bar stool by the kitchen. "Don't do that Ayaan."

"Is it because the baby won't be yours?"

Kenneth ran his hand over his head. "That's not it. I just never saw myself as a father."

Ayaan turned away from the window and faced Kenneth with her arms folded. "If I told you I was pregnant, would we be having a different conversation or would you be telling me that you don't want the baby growing in my belly?"

"That's a moot point."

"No, it's not a moot point. It's a valid point. If I told you it was a miracle and the doctors lied and I'm carrying your child, would we still be having this conversation?"

"Ayaan, please. That's not the point?"

"It is the point. It's my point. I want to know if I was pregnant with your child, would we have this same conversation?"

"Ayaan, we have options. We don't have to have a child. I know that's what couples do. They get married and they have children. We don't have to. We don't have to do what other people do. We can do what we do. We can work and travel and experience life in a way that you can't with children."

"So if I were carrying your child, we wouldn't be having this conversation. That's what I'm getting by your lack of an answer."

"I guess if you could have children, we would have talked about it."

"But since I can't have children, there is no need to really discuss it. It was just one of my projects. You didn't take it seriously."

"I just didn't think we'd have to deal with it this quickly. I thought I'd have time to get used to the idea."

"There is nothing for you to get used to. You're packed. The plane leaves at 7:00 p.m. tomorrow. I expect you to be there. Since you love me and all, prove it. Go with me to France, and let's get our child. You have options; I have only one. I'm getting on the plane for France. I can't get that baby without you."

Kenneth's voice cracked, and he asked, "Can't we even discuss it?"

Ayaan looked him square in the eye. "You just need to get your mind right. We have an interview to rock."

"I didn't say we'd never have kids. I just … it's just within two months. That's quick. I just … open adoptions, France, it's just … Ayaan, I love you. Let's talk about it. Not fight about it, but really talk about it. Let's figure it out together."

"You have already figured it out. You probably started falling in love with me the minute you found out that I was half a woman, the half you needed, the twat part. You only wanted the part that could ride you half the night. You only wanted the part that could suck you off. The uterus was extra. What the fuck is a fallopian tube? Fuck that shit. You like spewing your seed in me knowing it will never fertilize an egg. You got off easy. I didn't."

Ayaan began stalking across the room. "It kills me that I can't carry your baby. It bothers me that I know you're spewing into an empty shell. I know this won't be your baby … I can't do that. I would do it happily if I could. I would lie in bed for nine months cultivating your child if I could. I can't."

Kenneth threw up his hands. "You're not even listening to what I'm telling you. You haven't heard a word."

Ayaan stopped stalking in front of him. "Are you going to Paris?"

"Ayaan, can we please talk about this?"

"Are you going to Paris?"

"Ayaan, let's—"

"Kenneth. Explain."

"I work all the time. My dad worked all the time. I don't want to be a parent like him. To do what we want to do, it'll take time. It'll take a commitment. I love working. I love what we do. If I was going to have a child, I'd want to do it full on, not half-ass. We're still so new. We have time."

"Don't you get it, Kenneth. We have *now*. Today. Tomorrow isn't promised. I know that better than anyone."

"Ayaan nothing is going to happen to you or me or us. We have all the time in the world."

"And what happens, Kenneth, if this is it—if this is our only chance and we frivolously throw it away. What happens then? I'll leave your luggage here in the morning. If you love me, you'll be on that plane." With that, Ayaan went to the bedroom and closed the door. She didn't sleep that night as hard as she tried. Her mind kept racing. Sometimes she cried. Other times her eyes would be bone dry. She prayed that Kenneth would be on that plane. If he was, everything would be all right.

Ayaan never planned on going into work that day. Kenneth was already gone by the time she woke up; his luggage was still at the apartment. Ayaan puttered around the house for a while, hoping that

Kenneth would call or show up. He did neither. She still had some errands to run before going to the airport, so she left a bit early.

Although she wasn't particularly religious, she was very spiritual. Before she left the house, she actually prayed over the luggage, that it would make it to the airport and Kenneth would make the trip with her.

Without him, there wasn't a trip really. They both knew that. In this case, he held the cards. If he didn't go, if he didn't rock the interview, they'd lose this opportunity. *Who knew when another one would appear?* The girl was interested in them. She wanted them to raise her child. At least potentially, that was such a blessing. *How could Kenneth not see what a rare blessing that was?*

Ayaan got to the airport early. That was a bad idea. All she could think about was whether Kenneth was going to join her or what would happen if he didn't. Would she still get on the plane? Would she do the interview herself?

The girl was adamant that she wanted her baby to grow up in a stable household with a mother and a father. *If the father didn't show up to the interview, how would that appear stable?*

She also wanted the parents to have college degrees and jobs. She had even asked for college transcripts. This girl was serious about the parents for her child. She also wanted an open adoption. She was only asking for pictures and the knowledge of where the child lived. She wanted to ensure that she didn't lose complete contact. She wanted to be certain that the baby was OK.

Ayaan continued to pace as they were calling the flight number. Kenneth was a creature of habit. He habitually showed up at the airport at least an hour before the flight was called. He missed a flight once in his life and refused to be in that position ever again. That he wasn't there, didn't bode well.

Ayaan sat down and put her head in her hands. *What was she going to do? Did she get on the flight? Did she go back home? Did she give up her dream of having a child?* She couldn't. She couldn't live with an empty life. She couldn't do it.

They gave the second call for the flight. Ayaan got up. She had hours to figure out a second plan. She'd have … as she looked up, she saw Kenneth rushing toward her. She let a whoop and rushed toward him. He dropped his luggage, so he could catch her as she launched herself into his arms.

This time she hung on with desperation. Then she pulled back and looked into his eyes. "You came."

"What can I say? I'd do anything for you. You should know that by now."

"You're right. I should." She looped her arm around his and walked to pick up her luggage so that they could board the plane.

On the flight, it was as if the stress had gone out of Kenneth. He was convinced that they needed a more comfortable bed in the guest room at some point. Either that or during the next argument, she was going to have to sleep there. He joked and then laughed. It was as if their relationship was back on track. They were on their way to fight for the right to raise this child.

After their plane landed the next morning, they ran to check into the hotel. Ayaan wished they could have left earlier. This was crazy to hop off an airplane, freshen up in the hotel room for a few hours, and then rush to the lawyer's office. They did it, though.

Ayaan paused outside the door of the lawyer's office. Looking at the wooden double doors, she suddenly experienced stage fright. *What if … God. What if? What if she said the wrong thing? What if they didn't like them? What if Kenneth jumped up again with the whole "he didn't want a child" discussion? What if everything?*

Kenneth had walked through the door. As he paused to hold the door for her, he turned around. He came out again and kissed her on the cheek. He looked her in the eyes and smiled at her. He took her hand and squeezed it. "Come on, babe. Who could say 'no' to us? We make Batman and Robin look like Tweedle Dee and Tweedle Dum."

Ayaan let out a small, nervous laugh. She allowed him to guide her across the threshold. She kissed him gently on the lips. "Thanks."

They walked through the door hand in hand and noticed a very pregnant girl at the top of the steps watching them. She lowered her gaze and hustled into an office. They looked at each other and followed her to the lawyer's office. Ayaan hoped her hesitation wouldn't work against them.

When Ayaan walked into the conference room, the girl was standing, gazing out of the window. When she looked up, Ayaan was stunned by three things: She had the saddest eyes she'd ever seen, there was a broken heart hidden in those eyes, and there was also a resolute tilt to the chin.

They sat down and the questions from the lawyer began.

Shelia

1997

Shelia thought she had mastered "alone." She thought she had it hands down. Really, she spent most of her childhood alone. Mother was always working or out somewhere or coming up with one new scheme after another. She was always reaching for something beyond her daughter and the motherhood that came way too early.

Shelia grew up with some friends, but none of the kind that stick forever. She never had the kind that you share your thoughts and dream with. She had the kind that you occasionally went to the movies with. She had the kind that wrote KIT in the yearbook, but never really meant it. The minute they separated, the friendship was forgotten.

Now, as she sat in this tiny Parisian apartment, she knew that she didn't know shit about being alone. It was dark outside, and Zel was at another shoot or appearance or something. Shelia was relieved she was gone. As she was growing, Zel was getting more and more excited about the baby. She even named the baby Sophia. It didn't matter that Shelia hadn't even found out the sex of the baby. She said that God wouldn't give two divas a boy to raise; dating them was bad enough.

Mama T was dealing with Mother at home, which, God bless her, had to be an ordeal in itself. At the same time, Mama T had called around when they decided to stay and found this apartment. She had a friend who was going to be primarily in the States for a few years; since she was paying the mortgage anyway, Shelia and Zel got to stay pretty much rent-free for just house sitting.

Shelia swore it was the size of two dorm rooms back home. However, at least there was a separate bedroom and the furniture was included. Without rent to worry about, Zel could easily afford their utility and hospital bills. The latter were quite reasonable, given the French health system.

It was as if everything—including the adoption—was falling into place. She had interviewed some couples, but she wouldn't make her final decision until she met the couple from the States. They were entrepreneurs or something to do with videos. She was a bit older than he, and she couldn't have children. Shelia thought that's what caught her eye.

Well, the first thing that snagged her attention was the fact that they were from Chicago. That would be convenient when she went back to the States. She wanted to make sure her child was OK. The whole purpose was to give her child a better life than it could have with her. *What was the point, if she dropped the kid off and never knew if it had it better than what she could have offered it?*

That was why she insisted on an open adoption. She didn't want to intrude on the child's life; she just needed to know that he or she was happy. Having this roommate in her body was more than Shelia had expected. The baby was kicking and moving; it was a part of her day. She made decisions about eating, exercising, just being based on what was good for the baby. She was going to lose that.

At least the baby would be with people who were ready for a child. They could be "in the moment" with the baby. The baby wouldn't be an afterthought. Being an afterthought was … well, difficult. Some things in life happen before a person is ready. Shelia probably hadn't been ready to have sex. Goodness knows she wasn't ready for the consequences.

But maybe, if she gave her baby to someone who would welcome it to their home, someone who would build a life around it, she would be doing something good. Shelia would no longer be a stupid girl who didn't listen to all the warnings about unprotected sex. She would be a mature woman, who was strong enough to do what was best for her child; but looking out into the Parisian night, Shelia knew deep down, she was the former.

She thought long and hard about this decision and went over every scenario in her head. Zel would help her. She would support her. Even now, Zel was weaving tales about their future. The future pretty much had Zel supporting a family. *How was that fair to Zel?* Zel made sure her men wore condoms. She was now taking on the role of the father.

Shelia felt guilty about Zel and Rick. She couldn't take anyone else's emotions on her head. She just couldn't do it. This baby was going to be free of all of this. That she was sure of.

The first couple that she had seen was a smart Parisian couple. They were lovely and friendly, but they almost didn't seem real. She couldn't get a good read on them. The second couple was from the States. They seemed pleasant enough, but she wasn't sure they were right either.

She wasn't looking for the perfect couple, but she knew the right couple had to be there. She'd hate to put these couples through this and not pick any of them. She didn't want to start from the drawing board.

The last couple was not only from Chicago, but his name was

Kenneth. That was Rick's middle name. It was almost kismet. Only Zel knew that Rick was the baby's father. The adoption system frowned on live fathers not giving up their parental rights. Dead fathers were easier. So Jacques Durant became the father of her child. They had gone to school together. He was clearly dead. It wasn't as if anyone was going to exhume the body to do a DNA test.

She was hopeful about them. She hoped that the fact that they were entrepreneurs meant that they could dedicate time to her child. That would be important. The child shouldn't have to struggle and hustle with the parents.

The child should be free to be a child.

Shelia turned away from the window. A teenager, even one as old as she, needed to be a teenager. She couldn't be a mom. Hell, she didn't know how.

She had this argument with herself, over and over. Zel and she had discussed motherhood at length. Zel was confident because her single-parent experience had been so different. Shelia couldn't comprehend a life where you go to work with your designer mother. When the schedule had been flexible, her mother could pick her up from school. All of that didn't compute.

All Shelia could see was Rick and she struggling to keep a roof over their heads and clothes on their child's back. She could see them tag-teaming: one working days and the other working nights and shuttling the child between them. She didn't have a degree or any skills. Hell, she didn't even know what she wanted to get a degree in.

He was in school on a basketball scholarship, working on a degree in political science. She had no idea what one did with a political science degree. Was that really in high demand?

Although his grades were decent, it wasn't as if he was a genius. *If they didn't have degrees that were in demand, what would they do? Would she find a cushy job as an administrative assistant somewhere?* Crap. Her frustration caused her to tug at her hair. There was no way around this decision. Everything was already in motion. She and the dead father were putting this baby up for adoption.

Walking to the kitchenette, Shelia opened the refrigerator. There was milk. There was always milk. Zel insisted on it. Shelia hated milk, but managed to choke down one glass a day for her guest. She felt restless. She went to her underwear drawer in her bedroom and pulled out some chips and a chocolate bar.

Zel had all but banned sweets from the house. She had to keep her model figure, and she had a bigger sweet tooth than the law allowed. So Shelia had to sneak in the contraband items, and hide them when Zel wasn't around.

She opened the bag of chips, ate a few, and then put a paper clip on them. She thought about putting them back just like that, but instead went and got a zip-closure bag. They'd stay fresher that way. She put the chips back in her drawer. She threw the candy bar in the garbage and covered it with the scrunched up paper towel she'd used to wash the salt from her hands. She just didn't feel like eating it. It served no purpose.

She walked into the bathroom and opened the medicine cabinet. She took her temperature for the fun of it and then tried to get engrossed in television. However, since she didn't speak fluent French, it was difficult to keep up with plot lines. She usually read books for entertainment, but she couldn't even concentrate on that. If this next couple didn't knock her socks off, she would have to start from the beginning. All the couples presented to her seemed OK, but they didn't stand out in any way. This was the biggest decision she ever made. It had to be right.

Zel was already trying to travel less, to be around Shelia more. The more Zel was around, the fewer opportunities Shelia had to interview prospective parents. Hell, she was still trying to work out with the doctor how she was going to induce childbirth while Zel was out of town.

Zel was spinning fairytales. Shelia wanted to believe in the fairytales so badly. She wanted to believe in the prince that would come to the rescue. She wanted to believe the beast would turn into a prince. She wanted to believe in happily ever after. However, those princesses kept their legs closed until the prince fell in love. There has yet to be a knocked-up princess. Hasn't happened, or at least she'd never heard about it. To hear Zel talk about it, they could make it work.

Shelia decided to go to bed. She lay there with her mind racing, trying to figure out how she was going to make all of this work. Eventually, she must have fallen asleep because she woke up and the sun was streaming into the apartment. She took her time and fixed herself an egg-white omelet. She was just about to sit down to eat when Zel called.

"Hey there, mama."

"You know I did have an identity before I became a baby storage unit."

"Yeah, but I like calling you mama."

"I take it you're on set."

"Yeah, it's hella' busy, but we're making it work."

"Any cute guys?"

Zel laughed. "Tons of cute guys. All oiled up and ready to go. With the amount of oil they use, you'd think we'd be doing straight porn."

"Anyone worth dating?"

"Who knows? I'm not even thinking about who. I'm trying to work here."

"So, you aren't dating anyone on set?"

"Sweetie, I don't date every single man that crosses my path."

"I'm pregnant. Not you. You should be having fun. You don't really go out. You hang around all the time with me. That can't be your life."

"Hanging around with my best friend beats half of these losers."

"OK, what about the other half?"

"Enough already. I have to get going. Place the phone by

Sophia. I have a secret to tell her."

"It better be clean. Hold on."

As she moved the phone to her belly, Shelia could hear Zel laughing. After they disconnected, Shelia started to get ready. She wore one of Zel's designs. It was a deep purple number, with an empire waist to accommodate the baby bump. Zel hated the simple clothes that Shelia had purchased, so she created a whole different wardrobe. Sometimes she even used material from the simple dresses.

Shelia knew she was dressed well. She pulled her hair back in a clip. She was only trying to look neat and presentable. She was interviewing them, not the other way around.

She pulled up to the lawyer's office and took a deep breath. She thought that it would get easier. She thought each interview would go more smoothly. The truth was there was not an easy part to any of this.

She often didn't sleep well, which would have been fine if it was due to the baby. She didn't sleep because her mind kept racing and wouldn't stop. Television didn't help. Music was useless. There was nothing to stop the constant badgering of her conscience that was constantly on her to share her story. It was needling her to call Rick, tell Zel her plans, ask Mother for help.

The problem was, her conscience didn't give an answer to "what then?". What was the next step after she told everyone what she was planning? It didn't mean that she wouldn't end up in the same place. The only difference would be that a lot of other people would be as hurt and disappointed as she was.

Shelia slowly made her way up the steep, narrow staircase to the lawyer's office. She always took her time on this particular staircase. She didn't want to slip and fall, since the only thing to catch her fall was marble. Something told her that wouldn't make a soft landing.

As she reached the top of the stairs, she heard the door open. She looked down to see a man walk through. He was wearing jeans, a suit jacket, and a nice button-down shirt. She couldn't see his face, but the top of his hair was trimmed close enough for her to see the bald patch at the top. He was solidly built and was holding the door open for someone who didn't walk through.

She heard mumbled conversation. He walked back aside. When he came through the door seconds later, he was holding a hand. They stopped in the threshold and kissed. The woman looked up and smiled at him. There was something in that smile, the clasped hands—in that body language. There was love there. It was the love that she didn't know existed. That woman was the princess.

The woman looked up the stairs, and they locked eyes for a second before Shelia broke contact to go to the lawyer's office. Shelia hustled herself into the conference room and stood by the window; she needed a moment to collect her thoughts. She knew that any minute now the Travers would come through that door and the interview would begin.

Her mind kept replaying the kiss and the look. She decided that was what the other couples were missing. It was hard to see or detect with the lawyer present, but there was a kind of intimacy in the Travers' relationship. Having witnessed it, Shelia knew without a single question being asked that she had found her child's parents.

She didn't feel relieved at the news. She felt a bit sadder. Each day, each decision was a countdown to the day that she would give her child away. That continued to weigh her down.

The Travers came in and sat down. She turned.

When Shelia sat down, there was still something rolling off the Travers in waves. It was in the way his thumb brushed her knuckles, in the way her eyes sparkled with a hidden secret when she looked at him, in the way their bodies seemed drawn to each other even as they sat in separate chairs.

Sometimes Shelia would lose her place in the conversation because she was busy watching them. As the interview wrapped up, Shelia held her hand out for a handshake.

Ayaan Travers hesitated for the barest minute. Then she pulled

Shelia into a hug.

Shelia felt the tightness in her chest and knew in minutes she'd be a blubbering mess.

Ayaan rubbed Shelia's arms and then stepped back.

As soon as the Travers left, her lawyer asked, "Well, what do you think about them?"

Shelia couldn't hold it together anymore. Tears were sliding down her face as she said, "It's them. They are my baby's parents."

"Are you sure? The first couple was more established and just as nice."

"It's them." Shelia hurried out of the office and started down the stairs. She stopped halfway down and sat on the stairs. This time with no one to witness it, she had the breakdown that she deserved. It lasted twenty minutes and left her exhausted. However, she knew she couldn't just stay in the hallway crying. Zel was coming home early tomorrow morning. She needed to pull herself together.

She walked back up to the lawyer's office. She needed to nail down the details now. She worked with her lawyer for another couple of hours. She waited in the conference room while he conferred with the Travers. She'd need a delivery date so that they'd know when to come back. However, they knew now that they had a baby.

Shelia found herself rubbing her stomach. This baby would be able to witness what she just had a glimpse of today. Maybe, this baby would one day experience a love that deep. When all was done, Shelia made her way back home.

AYAAN

1997-1998

Ayaan and Kenneth took the long way home. There was something about Paris that made them want to stroll. It was so different from Chicago. In Chicago, they scurried. They always had some place to be. Here, they were at the place they needed to be. Here, they could just exist.

They stopped at a little shop for croissants and tea. Of all the high-end teas available in the world, it truly surprised Ayaan that they would only have the option of Lipton. To Ayaan's palate, they might as well have offered her sewer water. Normally, she would have declined. This time, she merely laughed and said, "When in Paris, might as well do as Americans."

They had their snack, and they walked and talked about nothing of importance. The city had a relaxing effect. It was such a tourist city. The museums were crowded with people carrying maps. It was easy to tell the tourists by the way they scurried everywhere.

Ayaan and Kenneth sat on a bench on the street in between the Arc de Triomphe and the Louvre, which are about three miles apart. That strip was busy and interesting. She laid her head on his shoulder. However, jet lag began to overtake her, so they headed back to the hotel. It was a good half-mile walk from where they were, but they didn't mind. When they arrived, they had a message waiting.

Ayaan looked at Kenneth. She didn't know if this was good or bad. Ayaan called back immediately. There are no words to explain the feeling deep in a woman's gut when the stick turns blue or the rabbit dies or whatever words they use to describe the fact that she's having a baby. A baby. In two months' time, Ayaan would complete her family.

She shrieked, jumped on Kenneth, and wrapped her legs around his middle. He spun her around. She jumped down and began to do a happy dance.

As she laughed and spun, she looked at Kenneth's face and stopped. She inhaled deeply before she said, "You're going to be a great father."

"Ayaan, I'm just not sure that I want to."

"Really? Really!" Ayaan threw up her hands. "Why did you come? Why did we come? She specifically requested a family. Without you … without you … I can't have my baby."

"I'm here. I'm with you. We can work this out."

"How can you not be happy about my baby?"

"It's not that I'm unhappy about it. I'm just not as excited about it as you are. Still I look at you, and I want to be so badly."

Ayaan sat down on the couch. "Want to be?" She placed her head in her hands. "Want to be?"

Kenneth walked over, kneeled down by Ayaan, and pulled her arms down. "Baby, we're going to have a child."

"Not if we're not all in. If we, meaning both of us, aren't all in, she's going to the next name on the list."

Kenneth played with her hand. "Would it be so bad? Would it be so bad if we passed on this baby? This isn't the last baby in the world. Next year, next year we could try again."

Ayaan looked at their joined hands. "Why wait when we can have a baby now?"

Kenneth nodded. "Then, we'll have a baby now. "

Ayaan looked at Kenneth skeptically. "How can you go between saying we'll wait to let's do it? It's a child. There is no return policy on a child."

Kenneth grunted as he pushed up from his squat. "For me, it's simple. Whatever makes you happy."

"Really? 'Cause, I just feel this is our child. This is the one we were meant to have."

"Then by all means, let's have our child. Have you thought of names?"

"If it's a girl, how about Ayaan Junior? I heard Della Reese named her daughter after her. I always loved that."

Kenneth looked at her with so much love. "When are we going to hear the details about Junior?"

"Our lawyers are going to work out the details. Hopefully, we'll know by next week. You should know, though, she's asking for an open adoption. She wants to know where the child is and how she's doing."

"Did you see her today? She looked so fragile. Are you sure that's the best route to take?"

"It's our baby. I don't care if she needs a letter a day. I'll make it happen."

"So you're sure?"

"I'm positive, daddy. You can't tell me that doesn't have a good ring to it."

Kenneth pulled Ayaan off the couch into his arms. "You do realize when you say it there is a whole different context."

Ayaan threw her head back and laughed. She led Kenneth to the bed and they spent hours exploring the depths of what daddy would do to please mommy.

As they lay drifting off to sleep, Ayaan had the presence of mind to ask. "If you'll do whatever to make me happy, what do you want?"

"After that, you have to ask?"

Ayaan hit him on the shoulder and then snuggled deeper in his arms. "I'm serious."

Although her eyes were closed, she felt Kenneth shrug. "I just need you and I'm good."

Ayaan smiled. "It's us now. As long as you have us."

Kenneth kissed the top of her head, as she began to drift off to sleep.

Two months passed like two weeks. What was once their tiny office at the apartment became the tiny nursery. Their dining room now had a very small desk set up in the corner to hold their computer. Every room doubled as something. Ayaan wouldn't have it any other way.

They talked about moving, but as Kenneth put it, "Do you really want to move now?" He had a point. They barely made their timeline as it was. However, the baby's room was together before she made it home. Even though Ayaan threatened, they didn't name her Ayaan Junior. Shelia had asked if they could name her Kendall. Shelia said it made sense with her dad's name being Kenneth. Ayaan didn't mind at all. Kendall she became.

Ayaan would rather work than clean any day of the week but, she had scrubbed the house from top to bottom waiting for Kendall's arrival. Ayaan just wanted everything right for her daughter. She had heard about mothers nesting when they were pregnant. That instinct had kicked in for Ayaan with just one phone call; she became a mother in every since of the word.

Kenneth bore the brunt of it, of course. They still had to do their job, but now their conversation was all about the baby. It was about shopping for furniture, painting walls, whether or not to have a baby shower, rearranging a household, day care, etc. There were so many decisions to make. Every minute of the discussion seemed to energize Ayaan.

As pumped as Ayaan was, poor Kenneth was drained. He, of course, was responsible for all of the physical labor. He painted. He put up book shelves. He rearranged furniture. He put new furniture together. He got rid of old furniture. Then he was putting in a lot of time at the company trying to expand their reach. The weekend before they were going to get Kendall, he suggested a long weekend prior to Paris. He said they needed to reconnect. Ayaan didn't have that kind of time.

At the time, the flight to Paris was interminable. Each minute was like a second. She ended up taking some melatonin to fall asleep on the flight. She was strung so tight, but looking back, it was merely seconds. The trip to the hotel was cake. The wait at the hospital flew like water through a chute. When Shelia put Kendall in her arms for the first time, time stood completely still. She was swaddled so completely that she was merely a face in a cocoon. The purity and peace of that face captured Ayaan's heart. Even with the lack of sleep, the constant details, the nonstop pace of new parents, each breath Kendall took matched the beat of Ayaan's heart.

That first day, Kenneth would peek at Kendall; but when Ayaan held her out, he shook his head. He just stared at her in awe. Starting out in Paris, Ayaan did everything. She held Kendall. She changed Kendall. Fed Kendall. Kenneth eventually caught up though. He slowly began to to pick up the skills necessary to take care of Kendall. However, that first day, the first time, he had denied his daughter. Ayaan had been watching him ever since.

Now they were back in Chicago sitting in chairs across from each other. Kendall was sleep. Ayaan's feet were on the coffee table. Kenneth was merely staring at her from across the room. He smiled, and she realized she couldn't smile back. It was time for one of those talks that she avoided like it was a poisonous snake.

Noting her face, Kenneth stopped smiling. "What's wrong?"

"Nothing exactly is wrong. Something just isn't right."

Kenneth lifted his arms and sniffed. "It ain't me." Ayaan smiled.

"You know when I feel like the most beautiful woman in the world?"

"When you don't smell like spit-up."

"I'm being serious."

Kenneth exhaled. "No, I don't know."

Ayaan looked him in the eye. "When I look at you. When I see the way you look at me. I see myself reflected in your eyes, and I feel absolutely beautiful. That's why I don't worry when you leave the house. Well, I worry some because I know women have no shame and men have little control. Still sometimes there's a way that you look at me and I know from the look you love me."

Kenneth smiled. "It's because I do. What's wrong with that?"

Ayaan gave a half smile. "You look at me like that. You never look at Kendall like that."

"What are you talking about? I'm here every day with Kendall. I change her diaper, give her baths, play with her."

"Yeah, you do. But you don't ... how can I put this? You take care of her, but you don't marvel in her."

"So you're saying everything I'm doing isn't enough."

"I know you, Kenneth. I know your capacity for love and generosity of spirit. I know how your mind works. I'm your best friend and you surely are mine. You aren't engaged with Kendall like you are with me."

"How much more *engaged* can I be?"

"You could love her."

"Stop pushing, Ayaan." Kenneth leaned his head back and closed his eyes.

Stop pushing? It had been a month and he hadn't changed. He did a lot for Kendall, but he wasn't invested in Kendall. Not the way a father should be. Not the way her daughter deserved. *She could stop pushing. She could. Then what? They would go on like this. A little girl should be a princess to her father. She shouldn't be another little girl.*

Ayaan recalled her own childhood. Her dad was always responsible for Sunday breakfast. Ayaan loved the weekends when she would rush downstairs to the kitchen. Her dad would be there getting ready to fix pancakes, waffles, French toast, or some other delicacy. Ayaan always wanted to help.

Sometimes, if they were up really early, he'd teach her to play poker with toothpicks. Her mother wouldn't have approved at all. Ayaan loved the fact that they were sneaking one past her mother. Sunday morning was their time. Her father worked two jobs to make ends meet. It would have been easy for him to sleep-in on Sunday mornings. It would have probably made more sense, –but just knowing that every Sunday she could run down the stairs and he would be there in the kitchen waiting for her, made her feel cherished.

She guessed that's why she waited so long to get married. She didn't want to settle for any old thing. She saw her friends go through one guy after another. They were always waiting and hoping and often settling. She looked at Kenneth. *He's good enough.*

She had everything. She did. And all he kept asking was for her to be patient. If it was just her, she could. She was so close to having everything she could possibly want. He was there when they made the commitment to this child. He was well aware there was no turning back. If he couldn't love Kendall with all that was in him, Kendall would know. What would that do to her?

"Ayaan, I don't know what's wrong with you. I said I will be a father to Kendall. I am being a father to Kendall. What is your problem?"

"What if your just being a father isn't enough?"

"What the hell? There is no *just* in what I've been doing. I haven't been phoning in fatherhood. I've been right here the whole time. I've known you for how many years? Our love grew." Kenneth threw up his hands. "You fell for Kendall from the first day. I'm sorry I didn't."

Ayaan closed her eyes. He'd admitted it: He didn't fall from the first day. She knew that. Deep in her heart, she knew his love for Kendall was a shallow version of what it could be.

"Ayaan, we have a great life. It's just going to get better."

"Yeah. It'll be great until my daughter asks me why her father doesn't love her. Then it'll suck."

"You're exaggerating, Ayaan. She will never ask that."

"You think I haven't been doing my research. Some adopted children are fine. Others constantly feel inadequate because their biological parents gave them away. I don't want to couple that with anything or add anything else on top of that. She needs to be solidly secure."

"Ayaan, you're acting insane."

"Kenneth."

"Ayaan, I love you with everything in my being. You know that. Stop pushing me about Kendall. I take damn good care of her."

Kenneth was right. He was present. She didn't have anything to complain about as far as what he did for Kendall. Knowing him, he'd be there for her whole life. That's who he was. He would be a great father. She was tripping and she was pushing. She knew what he could be and that difference was huge. *Would it ever be that for Kendall? Would it even matter to Kendall if his world didn't light up when she entered the room?*

It should. In her own house, the world should stop turning for her. It was that one step that would put this whole family over the top. The other issue was that Ayaan hadn't planned on having just one child. As an only child, she always knew she wanted more than one. If Kenneth wasn't roots deep in love with Kendall, what would he say to others?

Ayaan had to push. If he couldn't love Kendall the way she deserved, could they stay together?

"Give her the rest of your heart. It's so big. So generous."

"Ayaan, calm the fuck down. Kendall is fine."

"She deserves better than fine."

"Really? How would you know what she needs and what I'm not providing and how she feels or will feel about it? You became a mother yesterday. Now, all of a sudden, you're an expert. Do you have a degree in child psychology? Are you a baby whisperer? Do you have ESP? Are you reading her mind? She is dry, fed, fat and happy, with a roof over her head. Now that's something we need to work on. We need to figure out a new roof situation, but everything else is fine. Stop making trouble where it doesn't exist."

"Don't dismiss me."

"Well, why not? You keep dismissing me. I keep telling you everything is fine and everything else will come in time. I don't even fuckin' know where this version of you came from, but this bitch is grinding my last nerve to a pulp."

"Now, I'm a bitch?"

"Right now, this instant, yes, you're a troublesome bitch, right now. Tomorrow hopefully will be better."

"There won't be a tomorrow."

"Shut up Ayaan and go to bed." So first he called her a bitch and then he told her to shut up. He now clearly didn't know who the hell she was.

"No, I will not shut up and go to bed. If you can't be a *real* father to my daughter, then you can't be *any* father to my daughter."

"Really? You're going to leave me. Why?"

"You don't love Kendall."

"I could treat her like a princess for the rest of her life and it wouldn't be enough for you. You don't want me more engaged. You want her to yourself. You don't want her to have a father. As I'm seeing tonight, you have enough balls for both roles."

Ayaan gave it time. She gave it six months. He still didn't take his relationship with his daughter to the next level. She got tired of arguing, so she shut down. He didn't know how important a father was to a daughter. He didn't get it, and he never would. He kept asking her what she wanted from him. He thought he was doing everything right.

Kendall should have what Ayaan had. Ayaan wasn't going to settle for half measures. Kenneth kept asking for "time," but they both knew, he might never get where she wanted him to be.

As much as she loved him, she loved Kendall more. She figured it would be easy to move out and start a new life.

It was easier. The distribution of property was amicable. Kenneth was more than generous with the business partnership.
She missed him. Every day. He was her first thought in the morning. He was her last thought at night. She constantly wondered what he thought about this or that. She would have thoughts in the middle of the day that she wanted to share.

Kenneth was a movie buff. They had watched both versions of *Imitation of Life*. There was a scene at the end when the maid was talking about the fancy funeral she wanted to have with horse-drawn carriages. They discussed how horse-drawn carriages were smooth as hell, but really impractical. Then one day she was driving down I-57 and she saw a horse trailer. On the back it said "Horse-drawn Carriages for Weddings." As she passed it, there was another sign near the front that read, "Horse-drawn Carriages for Funerals." Maybe elegance wasn't dead after all. She wanted to call Kenneth to tell him, but she had already called him once that week. Once a week was her limit—unless he called her.

Sometimes, they'd meet for dinner. Then they'd fall back into their old routine. Mostly. She made sure not to touch him. To touch him would mean to kiss him, and to kiss him would lead to him flat on his back.

She had a good life, still she knew as sure as she was standing there that she wanted to beg him to take her back. Kendall would have been fine. Ayaan was unraveling. She hadn't met any man in her life worth shining Kenneth's shoes. She always said she didn't need a man. Did that. She realized too late that Kenneth was her oxygen.

Zel

2003

Zel's flight landed in Chicago. Shelia didn't meet her at the airport. Hell, Shelia didn't know she was coming. Zel had decided to keep that little tidbit to herself. At the rate Shelia was going, she'd be hiding out in the airport bathroom. Mama T would have loved to pick her up. Zel had missed her mother so much.

However, priorities were priorities. Right now, Zel needed to get to Shelia. She needed to have a conversation that was a long time coming. Not another useless argument. They needed to lay a lot of things to rest.

Zel got her luggage and rented a car. As she eased the town car through traffic to I-294, Zel rubbed her eyes. She slept some on the plane, but it had been a fitful sleep. Since the flight to Chicago occurred through the day, most of the passengers stayed awake. People were constantly talking.

She had the unfortunate turn of luck to sit next to a man that was on his way to a convention. He had never been to Chicago. At first it was cool, she told him all about the city and the cool spots. After a while, though, she was done. He was still talking. Zel wanted to sew her ears shut. Actually, she wanted to shut his mouth with super glue. Then, she didn't want to be the rude American; so she tolerated it until she had thoughts of pulling her own nails out. Eventually, he went back in coach to talk to some friends and Zel was able to catch a couple of hours of sleep.

That wasn't enough. She was dragging. Hopefully, Shelia would have some type of caffeinated beverage. As she pulled into Shelia's driveway, Zel was duly impressed with the house. It was a beautiful brick house. There was actually a little land around it.

Zel walked up and rang the doorbell. No answer. This heifer didn't have anywhere to go. Zel rang the bell again. Shelia eventually came to the door in baggy jogging pants and a T-shirt. "Shut up. You weren't due 'til next week."

Zel posed. "Sometimes the best entrances are made early instead of later."

Shelia squealed, and they pulled each other into a tight hug.

Zel was the first to break away. She pulled back with tears streaming down her eyes. "Wow. You know I didn't realize how much I missed you until this very moment. I came up here all full of 'piss and vinegar' as Grandmamma T would say. Now, it doesn't matter. I'm just so happy to see you."

Shelia smiled. "Not surprising. You were born full of piss and vinegar. A little bullshit was added later." Shelia laughed. "But, hell, I don't care."

"Honey, grab a bag. Let's get out of the prying suburban eyes. I'm sure there has to be one biddy ready to start the rumor that your gay lover came over with bags full of goodies."

Shelia was still smiling. "You are such a city girl."

"Yes, I am. Now, I need a bath and a bed, in that order. As great as it is to see you, I'm in desperate need of sleep."

"I thought you were supposed to stay awake to get your body used to a new time zone."

"News flash. I've traveled enough to realize my body does not get used to new time zones. So lead me to the spare room."

Zel and Shelia dragged her luggage up to the spare bedroom that was furnished with only a bed, but it did have black-out curtains on the window.

Zel gave Shelia a look.

Shelia shrugged. "You weren't due until next week, remember? At least there are black-out curtains, which you requested."

"Yeah. We'll talk later."

Zel took a quick shower, and when she came back to the room, there was a glass of warm milk on the nightstand. She drank it and snuggled under the covers. She closed her eyes and immediately went to sleep. When she woke, Shelia had left her a note saying she went to the store.

It was a good thing because as Zel looked through the cabinets, there wasn't a whole lot to choose from. Zel was suddenly ravenous, and her only options were eggs, toast, and spaghetti. Looking through the cabinets a bit more closely, there wasn't even sauce or tomato products to make spaghetti sauce. So she could have breakfast or spaghetti with butter. Shelia had to be keeping every take-out person in the neighborhood in business. They probably had her photo on the wall as customer of the month.

Zel fixed herself some eggs and toast, poured a glass of water, and went out back to the yard. She sat on the lounger on the patio and closed her eyes. It was peaceful out here in the back end of the world. Shelia's garden was in full bloom, so Zel made sure she sat down next to the bug repellent thingamajig. She hoped it worked effectively. She was just settling in when she heard a soft noise.

"Psst."

Zel tilted her head and looked around the yard. There wasn't anyone there. Thinking she was hearing things, she laid her head back on the lounger.

"Psst."

Zel whipped her head to the left. She could see the tiny eye of a child looking at her. Zel got up and walked over to the fence and knelt down.

"Hello."

"Shhh. I'm not supposed to talk to strangers, but you're in my neighbor's yard, so you're really not a stranger. I don't think Cleo would like it, though."

Zel started to whisper. "Is Cleo your mom?"

The eyeball giggled. "No Mommy is my mom. Cleo takes care of me. She used to babysit me, but I'm not a baby anymore."

"I can see that. Well, my name is Zel."

"Hi, Miss Zel. I'm Kendall. You sure are tall."

Zel smiled. "Thanks. I grew this way."

"Do you know the neighbor lady's name? If I know her name, then my mommy can't say she's a stranger."

"You mean Shelia."

"Thanks." The eyeball turned around and looked at the house.

"Does your nanny know you're out here?"

"We're playing hide and seek. I think she's still looking in the house. I hide really good when I want to."

Zel snorted as she held in a laugh. "Yes, I'm sure you do."

"I'm having a birthday party tomorrow. You should come. Bring Miss Shelia. I invited her, but she's so sad and crying all the time, I don't know if she's going to make it."

"You've seen her cry?"

The eyeball checked the house again. "Yes. In my driveway. My mommy talked to her, but I think she's still probably sad. She's been sad since she moved in. My party will help."

"Does your mommy know that you've invited people to your party?"

The eyeball tilted up thinking. "Well, she told me not to invite other people without asking her, but that was after I had already invited Miss Shelia. If you're a guest of Miss Shelia, you have to come, too."

They both heard the voice at the same time. "Kendall. Come on out."

"Oh. Tomorrow. You'll see the decorations. It's a huge party. I have to go." With that, the eyeball disappeared and Zel heard shuffling heading towards the neighbor's house.

Zel went back to her lounger smiling. She almost felt sorry for Cleo; she had her hands full. Clearly, this was a smart little girl.

Zel went into the family room and turned on the television. As much as she was used to France and even spoke French fluently, she missed American television. Fine, there were some shows she could watch. She spent a couple of hours watching mindless television. Then she must have fallen back to sleep. Next thing she knew, there were pots clanging in the kitchen.

She blinked and looked over at Shelia.

Shelia grimaced. "I didn't mean to disturb you. I just wanted to get dinner started."

Zel stretched. "No worries. I just keep falling asleep. As skinny as you've gotten, I thought that you had forgotten how to cook."

"Wow, right out of the gate. What happened to just missing me?"

"Ahh. That I do. If you were modeling, I could possibly understand it. But—"

"Well, we're having nice fattening pasta for dinner, so we'll both put on a few pounds."

Zel got up and walked to the kitchen. She sat at the island that separated the kitchen from the family room. There was now a bowl of fruit on the island, so she helped herself to an apple.

"Where's Devon?"

"He's working late. He had planned on taking a couple of days off when you came to town. He wanted to hang out with us a bit."

"I thought he hated the ground that I walked on."

"No, he knows you hate the ground that he walks on. He doesn't mind you, but he thought he'd give getting to know you a shot."

"Does he know that I want you to move to Paris with me?"

"No—and you aren't going to tell him either."

"Spoilsport."

"So really what gives? You've been crying and depressed since you moved in."

Shelia whipped her head around. "Who told you that?"

"The little neighbor girl, Kendall."

Shelia put her head back down and started cutting tomatoes for the spaghetti sauce. "So do you like your sauce spicy?"

"You know how I like my sauce. Why are you crying all the time? Why are you crying in the neighbor's driveway? Why are you losing weight? Is it hormones? Are you pregnant?"

Shelia looked incredulously at Zel. "No, I'm not pregnant."

"Are you sure?"

"Listen, I wasn't before we left the city, and we haven't gotten down like that since the move. So, yes, I'm sure."

Zel walked over and took the knife out of Shelia's hands. She thought it would be better if sharp objects were removed from the immediate vicinity for the talk they needed to have.

Zel dragged Shelia into the family room. "OK. Devon is at work. It's just you and me. We have a lot to sort out. To begin with, I'm seeing someone."

Shelia's eyes were suddenly wide open. "Is it forever, ever?"

Zel cringed. "He wants it to be. He asked me to marry him."

Shelia bounced in the seat, clapping. "You're getting married."

"No, I'm not. I can't. It's not right. It's OK, but it's not right. I don't know how to make it right."

"Is it Jacques?"

"It is and it isn't. It's the fact that I know what it could be. What Paul and I have isn't it. It's good and it's close. If it wasn't for Jacques, I might have been able to do it. Since I had Jacques, I don't think I can. It does feel good, though. It feels great to have someone to come home to. It feels great to have someone with whom to share your thoughts and feelings. It feels great having him there. It's like a comforter. However, there's no spark to it. It's just comfortable."

"Oh, Zel. Maybe that's good enough."

"Yeah, well maybe. Tell me what's going on with you. Remember, you called me and told me you were going to deal with the stuff in your life."

Shelia took a deep breath. "I shouldn't have moved here."

"Are their ghosts? What's the deal? Is this one of those houses like in the movies? Is the television going to come on without the remote?"

"Listen. I don't need any other issues to deal with. No and no. And now I'm not going to be able to sleep at night listening for creaking floorboards."

"Baby, you're so unhappy. I see it and I've only been here for a minute. The neighbors apparently know."

"I moved here thinking that I was strong enough to face my demons. Not my demons, but my decision. It wears on me every day."

"Is it that your neighbor has a daughter around Sophia's age?"

"No." Shelia took a deep breath and finally looked Zel straight in the eye. "It's the fact that my neighbor has my daughter. She *is* Sophia. Well, she's Kendall—but Kendall is Sophia."

Zel didn't move. She couldn't. Her breath was shallow. Her wish, her dream. Sophia was next door. Zel got up, walked to the patio and out the door.

Shelia jumped up as Zel was going down the patio steps. She grabbed her arm and dragged her back into the house. She closed and locked the patio doors. She pushed Zel toward the family room couch. "Where the hell did you think you were going?"

"I don't know. I just—"

"Kendall doesn't know she's my daughter. Apparently, she just thinks I'm some crazy neighbor lady who can't stop crying."

"What about her mother?"

"Shit. I've been avoiding Ayaan since I moved in. I know she wants to talk, too, but how can I explain what I don't know myself? This isn't what we agreed to. This isn't what she signed up for. I wasn't supposed to show up out of the blue. Yet, I did. Seeing Kendall

... seeing her hurts. I want to grab her and run off. She's so happy and feisty and determined. She's not me. She's better. I think she's better because of Ayaan. What can I offer her that's better than what she has?"

"You can offer her you. You're her mother. Anything else you need you know I have. I've been thinking about this for years. Rick never gave up his rights. He could get her back."

"Whoa. What are you trying to do to Kendall? Now, she'll have two parents that she didn't know about and a media storm to boot. Are you serious? He's a basketball player. There is no sliding this under the rug. You promised. You've kept the pregnancy and the daddy from everyone all these years. That's it. No press. No press means no Rick. I know now what I did was wrong. At least the way I did it was wrong. No two ways around ir, but I honestly think that would be worse.

"Did you hear what I said? She's happy. I was at my bedroom window one day and I heard her laughing in the yard. It's not something I could take back. I gave her away. Without Rick's knowledge, I signed the papers. That's not something I can take back. Every day I want to though. Every day I know I can't. I fight it every day. I suppress my feelings. I push them deep so that I don't do anything stupid and ruin a little girl's life—and not any little girl, my little girl.

"My stomach is a big knot all the time. It started to ease today when you came, and that's when I started cooking. Now, it's in a big knot again."

Zel took Shelia's hands. "We could make it work."

Shelia pulled Zel into a hug. "You always say that. It is working. It's working like it's supposed to. The only problem is me. If I hadn't moved in next door—"

"Yeah. Why the fuck would you do that? Wait, first, I can't believe you didn't tell me that you knew where Soph ... Kendall was all along. I won't forgive you for that one. Why the hell are you next door? Killing yourself with pills or exhaust fumes like everyone else was too pedestrian for you. You had to torture yourself to death."

"I'm not dying. Since we were moving, I figured why not

the south suburbs. When Devon liked this house, it was like a sign. Unfortunately, the sign may have said 'Do Not Enter.' I might have misinterpreted."

Zel snorted.

"Don't worry. We're going to move."

"How do you propose to get Devon to agree to that?"

"Easy, give him what he wants. Get pregnant. If I get pregnant, he'll give me whatever I want."

"Can you handle that?"

"In case you didn't notice by my skeletal frame, I'm not handling anything well right now, but I still wake up in the morning. I don't tell my daughter that I'm her mother. I go back to sleep. That is probably my biggest challenge to date. I haven't done it well, but I've done it. I think part of the problem is not knowing if I want her back or not. That's what put the knot in my core. As we talk about it, I know my time has passed. It hurts. I mean hot branding iron to the forehead hurts, but I think I can live with it."

"So there's a party tomorrow?"

"Yes, we're going. I'm going to look at her up-close and say goodbye and put Ayaan out of her misery. That lady is amazing. I would have put sugar in my gas tank by now."

Zel laughed. "Shit. She probably thought about it and figured if you couldn't drive, you couldn't leave."

Shelia got up and went back to cutting tomatoes. "Come on and talk to me about something good. Tell me about Mama T. She's always good for a story."

Zel and Shelia talked into the night. They talked about open and taboo topics. Devon came home and went to bed. They were still talking away. They were college-talking, with all the ghosts of their past, weaving a tapestry of a shared history. They got back to who they had been six odd years earlier.

AYAAN

2003

There was nothing more exhausting than planning this party for Kendall. She didn't know how many people were coming, thanks to Kendall's proclivity for inviting perfect strangers to her house. Every time she turned around someone else was saying how they would see her at the party. You'd think Kendall was twenty-one instead of five and a half. All Ayaan really wanted were the kids from the play group. They were manageable and no stress.

Instead, now she was playing host to kids from the play group, the park, the store, and who knows where else. To top it off, she found out Kenneth was coming. He said that if Shelia was going to show up, he wanted to be there for moral support. *However, who's going to provide moral support for him? No one.* She was stressed about the party, stressed about the guest list, stressed about unwanted visitors and now stressed because she decided to come to the beauty salon on a Friday night.

Friday night appointments were only trumped by Saturday morning appointments. Either way, she wasn't getting out of there anytime soon. She might as well have brought dinner or she could do like their particular hairdresser, she could take a break from finishing a five-year-old's hair to peruse the menu.

However, it wasn't just looking at the menu that was the problem. The hairdresser looked at the menu, then she went to the shampoo bowl to discuss it. Then she talked to another patron for a while. Twenty minutes later she put in her order. That didn't include the break for the phone calls, conversations, and anything else she could think of.

After a while, Ayaan could tell Kendall was at the end of her rope; she'd already figured there was no way this lady was getting a tip. She wouldn't get paid at all, if Ayaan found someone else to finish Kendall's hair and they had to walk out of there with Kendall's hair all over the place.

Ayaan was trying to figure out a solution that didn't include having to do Kendall's hair herself. It was Kendall's birthday and it should be special; her styles were not birthday party spectacular. Ayaan didn't feel like arguing with Kendall over hair. They were both tired enough and stubborn enough for that to have a bad ending.

Ayaan was on the phone calling her friend to see if she was available to finish Kendall's hair when she saw Kendall climbed out of the stylist's chair.

She walked over to the stylist and tapped her on the leg.

The stylist looked down and met eyes with Kendall.

Kendall pointed to the chair as if to tell the stylist she needed to get her tail in gear.

The stylist looked shocked, but she followed Kendall back to the chair and finished her hair.

Ayaan smiled.

Although she had taught Kendall to respect her elders, she kind of got a kick out of the fact that Kendall was smart enough to know this lady was not doing her job. Her baby put a grown stylist in her place. She couldn't wait to tell Kenneth about that. It was perfect timing because she would see him tomorrow.

The party had to be perfect. She had a lot to prove to a lot of people. Thinking about it, she should have hired a party planner. No, she had to be super mom. People assumed because she worked at home she had all kinds of time.

However, she found she had less and less time. She didn't have a staff that she could delegate to; it was all on her. When she had to put together a proposal, it was her name and reputation on the line. It wasn't anyone else's. She had to meet her deadlines and promote the business as well. It was a lot of work.

On top of that, she was a party planner. The house was clean. She had ordered the Jumping Jack. She had hired someone to grill hot dogs and hamburgers. She thought about having a petting zoo, but she realized she wasn't that kind of mother. She didn't have the patience for animals. Instead, she went with a carnival theme with a lot of child-friendly games in her back yard. The kids could go from station to station and play. She even picked up a load of prizes from the dollar store. She just had to remember that it was only three hours. Kids in and then kids out.

Kendall was still sitting in the chair mean-mugging the hairdresser. When the stylist finished Kendall's hair, Ayaan hadn't changed her mind about no tip. When a five-year-old had to put her in her place, clearly she didn't earn a tip.

Kendall went to bed that night without argument. Ayaan stayed awake in the dark looking at the house next door. The lights were still on at 10:00 p.m. She still wondered what Shelia really wanted. She hadn't spoken to her since Shelia had tried to park in her driveway. She knew eventually they were going to have to really talk.

The problem was she couldn't even blame Shelia for this all the way. She was terrified to speak to Shelia. As much as she made resolutions and talked to lawyers and the like, truth was, she didn't know what she was going to say if Shelia said she wanted to get to know Kendall. The first thing the lawyer asked when she called was what did Ayaan want to do. The reason she hadn't spoken with her lawyer since was because she didn't know. She said she wanted Shelia stuck at the top of the Eiffel Tower; but the truth was, Shelia was still Kendall's biological mother.

Shelia had given Ayaan this gift. Ayaan wasn't ready to give Kendall up. She didn't know if there was something in between that she could work with. Truth be told, she would probably always be a bit afraid of Shelia. Fear alone couldn't direct this decision. Kendall had to trump all adult thoughts and feelings on the subject. What would work for Kendall? What wouldn't ruin the secure cocoon that she had put her daughter in?

Thinking about how this party was shaping up, Kendall wasn't comfortable in this emotional cocoon. Well, she was comfortable in it. It was her base. Ayaan had to admit, Kendall was going to continue to expand and push at her limits. She had spirit that Ayaan marveled at on a daily basis.

Kendall knew she had two mothers. She assumed it was like a stepmother like some of her friends had. She kind of took it in stride that she never saw the parents that were responsible for her birth. Ayaan figured it was because Kendall was always two steps ahead of everyone including herself.

What would happen if her biological mother appeared? That was a stupid question. She had appeared. She appeared and Kendall felt sorry for her because she couldn't stop crying. She already had Kendall's sympathies.

The thing that Ayaan held on tight to was the fact that she had Kendall's love. It wasn't just because she was her mother. They had fun together. They loved spending time together. They loved going to the park. They loved reading together. They loved dancing in the playroom. Sometimes, they would just lie together and exist.

How much of that would be upset when she had to share her

with Shelia? If she had to share her with Shelia. Shelia still hadn't told her what she wanted. Ayaan went to bed every night praying that Shelia would disappear as easily as she appeared. One night she tried clicking her heels three times. In the morning, Shelia's husband's car still left the garage at the same time.

There was a new car in the driveway tonight. It was rental. Ayaan had taken it upon herself to walk around the block to check it out. There was a time when she thought she was above stalking. Apparently, she just never had a reason to stalk before.

She definitely didn't stalk Kenneth. She was afraid she would find something. It was bad enough that if he wasn't available when she called and he didn't call back in a timely manner, she'd get pissed off. Then she'd be more pissed off because she couldn't ask him about it. She figured if she saw some skank coming out of his place, the place they used to share, it wouldn't be pretty.

Now she was skulking around her neighbor's house. She was sad. She had thought about telling Kendall about Shelia. It would be easier than sitting here waiting for Shelia to drop a bomb. Kendall wouldn't just take it at face value and keep going about her business. Ayaan knew she'd need to interact with Shelia; the woman obviously wasn't stable.

Soon she'd have to tell Kendall something. She couldn't let Shelia do it. Kendall was her child, her responsibility. It wasn't as if Shelia was renting the house next door. She had purchased it. That meant she was going to be there for a while. It was better if Ayaan directed the conversation. It would be better yet, if Shelia packed her shit and left. In lieu of that, she'd have to take action. The stakes were too high. She could manage the conversation and still have to share her child. Ayaan turned away from the window. She had a big day tomorrow.

She awoke from a restless sleep and dragged herself out of bed. By the time the party started, she was still tired, but managed to dig deep and put on a cheery attitude. She had to for Kendall's sake. Now she was glad she did. The party was turning out well.

Shelia had brought her friend Zel, who was definitely a live wire. It was an infectious charisma that was entertaining the others. With the exception of a small wave that Shelia and Kendall exchanged when they first arrived, Shelia had stayed away. She seemed to be enjoying herself. Kendall definitely was. She hadn't stopped running.

Kenneth had met up with the only other guy there. Ayaan forgot his name, but he always accompanied his daughter to these events. He always looked bored out of his mind. However, when his daughter was around, there was a light in his eyes and a smile on his face.

She knew he was into martial arts, because he would occasionally do a few moves in between trips to the buffet. He was broad-shouldered and lean-hipped. Kenneth was also looking lean these days. She'd known him for years, and he kept that extra fifteen pounds. Now, when he pointed at something, a small mountain appeared on his bicep.

Ayaan went into the kitchen to bring out some more sandwiches for the buffet. She had help, but she was feeling a little anxious. When she came out, she realized her anxiety had a name. It was Shelia, who was standing next to Kendall looking like her twin, and she had the nerve to have a trembling lip as if she was about to cry.

Kendall, who was used to the crying neighbor, was patting her on the leg.

Shelia couldn't believe this latest meltdown at a birthday party in a yard full of parents, including her daughter's mother. All she could think about was, it was a good thing Devon was at work again/still.

Their relationship wasn't going to survive this move. She could feel it in her bones. They had been doing all right before they came out to the suburbs. Now she was falling apart, and she couldn't tell him why. In a minute, she was going to be in a white padded room eating Jell-O™ and apple sauce for every meal.

However, when she looked at Kendall, she saw Mother. She had seen her before, but this time she actually looked at her. Then

Kendall threw her head back and laughed. She had seen Mother laugh like that. *Hell, she had laughed like that.* She couldn't seem to hold it together. She had told herself she would. She had made a silent promise to Ayaan that she would. She had broken that promise—clearly. Now she was leaking all over the place. Her eyes, her nose. It was a disgusting site.

Ayaan rolled her eyes. She would kill her. Zel wasn't around, so Ayaan had to take matters in her own hands.

Shelia was a grown-ass woman getting consoled by a five-year-old. What the hell? Her own daughter was looking at her like she was a crazy lady. Not cool.

"Mommy?"

Shelia's breath caught. Did her daughter just … Then she felt Ayaan's presence over her shoulder.

Ayaan didn't even dare look at Shelia. At this point, she was torn between heartbreaking depression and violence. She didn't know which one was going to win out.

She turned to her daughter. "Shelia is just a bit sad. I'm going to take her inside for a little nap. You can go play with your friends."

Kendall looked torn. "Will you fix her tea and read her a book?"

Ayaan smiled. That was her girl. "Of course, I will."

With that, Ayaan dragged Shelia into the house.

Thank God. Kids didn't need to see this.

When Zel came out of the bathroom and saw Ayaan dragging Shelia across the patio, she was ready to cut someone. Then she saw Ayaan's resolve and Shelia's tears, and she was like shit on a stick. *For real?*

Ayaan stared her down. Zel had a good six inches on her, but, she could tell that Ayaan was ready to break her down. Zel knew she was a bad bitch, but Ayaan looked like she was ready to cut a hoe—and the hoe wasn't going to be Zel.

As they passed at the door, Zel asked, "What the hell?"

Ayaan looked her in the eye. "This is my daughter's party. I'm going to need you and weepin' willow over here to come with me."

A storm started to gather in Zel's eyes. "You don't have to manhandle her."

Ayaan hitched her head up higher. "Then you bring her, but we're going to have a nice long conversation, and the fact that we have to do this now is really pissing me off. Don't fu—" Ayaan took a deep breath and prayed for strength. "Don't mess with me."

Ayaan led them down the hall to her office, held the door open, waited for them to follow before she closed and locked it.

They took seats and just stared at each other. They all jumped a bit at a knock on the door.

She heard Kenneth's voice. "Ayaan?"

"I'm fine. I'll talk to you later."

She heard him shuffling with hesitation at the door. She blew out a loud breath, got up, and opened the door. She saw the question in his eye. "Listen, I need you to go back to the party. Eat. Drink. Be merry. Keep kids going to the bathroom and handle anything that needs to be handled. This is going to take a while—and no—you can't help."

For a while, Zel thought Ayaan was going to cut him. Zel couldn't be upset at that. If someone had to go down, that seemed like a good choice to her, but she just barked orders at him and sent him on his way.

That made Zel doubly glad she hadn't tangled with Ayaan, who rolled her eyes as she closed the door. She looked at Ayaan. "Your husband?"

Ayaan looked puzzled. "Ex." Then she turned to Shelia. "You weren't kidding when you said that no one knew anything about Kendall, were you?"

Shelia grabbed a tissue off of the desk. "No." When Kenneth knocked on the door, she thought for sure she was going to have to hide under the desk. She saw way he looked at Ayaan. He wanted to eat her up. He would slay dragons for her. The only dragon anywhere in the vicinity was Shelia, and she didn't want to get cut by an angry hubby. Ex-hubby—however, they were packaging it up and trying to sell it.

He still had that look that she'd seen the first day they had met. They were still in love. In that Shelia had been absolutely right. She never got the details about their relationship. She heard what Ayaan was saying, but she didn't buy it. His vibes reached over the snot and through the tears into Shelia's psyche. Ayaan could protest all she wanted, but he was still her man.

Shelia knew he wasn't going to tolerate all this bullshit, because he didn't want Ayaan to have to deal with it. When Ayaan sent him packing, Shelia was even more scared. He had to know how pissed Ayaan was. Now she was taking it out on him. Shelia was sure he was going to cut someone. Instead, he just walked away. Thank God. Ayaan's eyes were peeling her skin off of her frame. That stare made Shelia shiver. She didn't want to know what Kenneth's glare would do.

Ayaan turned to Zel. "Long story short: he didn't know if he wanted to be a father. I don't like ambiguity. So since he didn't know, I made the choice for him."

Zel looked over at Ayaan. *Yeah. She would have made that decision for him.* However, Zel knew men. The looks he gave Ayaan let Zel know that whether or not he knew he wanted to be a father, he knew for sure that he wanted Ayaan. It didn't take a rocket scientist to figure that one out. Shoot. Zel had overheard Kendall asking him about her mother. Even a five-and-a-half year-old figured out something more was up. She didn't know who Ayaan thought she was fooling.

Zel turned to look at Shelia. She knew this was a bad idea. This girl wouldn't know stability if it was tattooed to her left thigh. Yet, she thought it was a good idea to show up at this party. She told Kendall she would come. Yeah, like a promise to Kendall should trump her responsibility to Ayaan. Shelia was ignoring a very big fact. This woman took Kendall in and gave her a home. She was secure enough to let Shelia know where her daughter was—and Shelia was fucking this whole thing up.

This was too much. All this crying was getting on her damn nerves and resolving nothing. Unless someone was buying stock in Kleenex and getting paid for all this sniffling, it was going to end now.

Zel switched her focus to Ayaan. She liked what she saw in Ayaan, probably because Ayaan had just sent a man packing and was glaring at Shelia. Fine. She ruined a good party. Zel could go back to it if she wanted. She didn't have to sit here and take care of Shelia.

Zel got up and walked over to Shelia. "Pull yourself together."

Shelia started mumbling something irrelevant.

"No. Listen. We don't have the time, patience, or fortitude for this shit. You've had your crying time. Now is time for you to suck this shit up and pretend you're a grown-ass woman. Suck. It. Up. Now."

"But—"

"Now."

"I know but—"

"This woman has every right to throw you out on your ass and get a restraining order, because you've been acting like a crazy heifer since I've been here, and you've probably been acting like a crazy heifer since you moved here. If you want to be the crazy heifer, let her know. She can get the paperwork together now. If you can't see your daughter without crying, you can't see your daughter. Get that?"

Shelia glared at Zel. "That's not your damn decision."

"Shit. That's what I would do. And she looks to be a bit smarter than I am."

"This is none of your damn business, Zel."

"Oh now, a bitch wants to get swole. A minute ago, you punked out at a kiddie party. What was it? The Jumping Jack reminded you of bad times? Maybe it was the Dora piñata. Were you afraid that Dora was going to get hurt? Did the sugar from the cake bring you down?"

Shelia snarled at Zel. "I can't stand your ass."

"Yeah, you know you love me."

They looked at each other and laughed.

Ayaan looked ready to snap their necks. The way her hands were flexing at her side could not be good. So they stopped.

Zel looked over and raised her eyebrows. "Sorry?"

Ayaan didn't know where to start. "You can't be here."

Shelia looked down. "I know."

"I don't mean at the party."

"Yeah, kinda' figured that. I thought it would be better, but it's tearing me apart."

Zel could see where this conversation was going. Before it got there, she needed a few answers.

"OK, Ayaan, I know you're going to kick us out on our collective asses. I got that. However, before you do, do you mind if I get your ex's number? He's hot."

Ayaan glared at Zel. The room stilled. The children quieted. Zel swore the wind stopped blowing. The whole world shut down, and Ayaan said four words that didn't tolerate any argument: "He's not your type."

Zel held up her hands in surrender. "My bad.

Zel and Shelia gave each other a look. Zel sat down on top of the desk. "So you love him. He loves you—and yet, you aren't together. Do tell."

"I don't owe you an explanation."

That brought Shelia out of her pity party. "I gave my daughter to a couple. I wouldn't have signed-off on a single mom raising my daughter. You're doing a great job, but I'm curious if you pulled a bait and switch. You seemed like such an upright lady in the interview."

"How would you know? You barely spoke in the interview."

"I didn't need to. There is something about the two of you that fits so well. It's what they write books about. I swear I've never seen it before, and I've never seen it since."

Ayaan looked at her a bit. "Yeah. It was something."

Shelia and Zel said in unison. "It *is* something."

Ayaan walked over to the window. She didn't say anything for a while. "He kept asking me for time. He kept saying give me time to get used to the idea of having a baby. Even after she was here, he needed time. When I looked at him, I knew who I was. In his eyes, I was smart, funny, gorgeous, sexy. Do you know how it feels to be with a man that's in love with you? God, when I kissed him. Baby, it should be outlawed how good that felt.

"But I didn't get that same feeling when he looked at Kendall. My daughter should be her father's princess. I didn't want her to feel that she was lacking in some way because she couldn't see herself in his eyes."

Zel and Shelia stared at each other, trying to decide who would take the lead.

Shelia folded her arms. She figured Ayaan had enough to dislike about her. She didn't need any more reasons for Ayaan to kick her out of this house. Zel started this. That meant she held the short straw.

Zel threw up her hands. "Do you have any girlfriends?"

Ayaan looked puzzled. "Why would you ask that?"

Even Shelia laughed at that one.

"Someone should have told you that you don't let *that* go. He could have shoplifted a Rolls off the lot in broad daylight with a video camera rolling and you're response should have been, "Don't worry, baby. We'll get a lawyer. I got you."

Ayaan smiled. "It's not that simple."

"The hell. A second ago, you were about to commit murder over a phone number. You know that's some good shit out there. Don't pretend you don't."

Ayaan thought about her next words. "When I was growing up, my father was my hero. I knew I was someone because he made sure I knew the depth of his love. My freshman year in high school, I wanted a name brand purse like all the other kids had. We didn't have the money, but he knew a guy. So every night, he would bring me a different designer purse. I didn't want any of them. He bought Louis

Vuitton, MCM, whatever the guy had. I wanted Liz Claiborne. The guy didn't have Liz Claiborne. So he went to Marshall Field's and bought it for me. I loved him for that. Do you know I still have the last present he bought me? It was a winter coat with a fox fur collar. I loved that coat."

"Where is your father now?"

"He's dead."

Zel looked at Shelia again. She would be so much better at the softer shit.

Shelia remained mum.

Zel tried another path. "What wasn't Kenneth doing? Did he not change a diaper? Did he not wake up for morning feeding?"

"Oh no, he did all that. I don't think it was love; it was more like responsibility or maybe it was his love for me. I just didn't get the feeling that it was his love for her. I just didn't feel that from him."

"So, he was waking up in the middle of the night?"

"Of course. Kenneth wouldn't let me do that by myself."

Zel had reached the end of her rope. "What the fuck is your issue?"

Shelia smiled. This was going to be good.

"What the fuck is yours?"

"Shit. Right now it's a crazy bitch that has some sick Oedipus complex with her father, so deep that she can't see that she should be straddling that fine drink of water that is probably, as we speak, organizing fuckin' game time to give you time to get us straight.

"I'm sure your father was a great person. He's dead."

"You think I don't know that? Every time I look at Kendall, I know that. I wanted him to meet her. I wanted him to know her. Every day, I know that he's dead."

"Do you still wear the fox fur collar coat around?"

Ayaan scrunched her nose. "What the hell? I need a damn map to talk to you. It's old. It stays in the closet."

"Yeah, you need to retire this conversation like you did that coat. Tuck that dead man in the back of the closet, and stop trying to wrap your husband up in his carcass."

"That's gross. Obviously, you don't get it."

"Why? Because I don't know where the hell my father is? That's a minor distraction. Not something to build a life out of. Kenneth loves you. Of course he loves Kendall."

"He has to love her for her."

"Need I repeat myself. Organizing games. Listening to baby lectures."

"What baby lectures?"

"Your baby is lecturing him about dating you. She told him that he should be her daddy. Yep. Your baby said that. You're the only clueless mother out there. Everyone else knows. You better recognize it, because that man is hungry for you. Some other chick is going to suck him dry, and he's going to think he's in love with her because you're a stupid hoe."

"How dare you call me that!"

"A stupid hoe. Yeah. Because obviously you aren't seeing what I'm seeing. A smart hoe would have revisited the situation by now, pulled out a mirror, looked for some damn reflections, and wrapped that back up. A stupid hoe thinks that is going to stay around for her. Stupid hoe."

"You don't get it."

"I do. I was raised without that reflection shit you were talking about. However, guess what? I had a mama. She reflected enough for five daddies. Get that man."

"I don't need a man."

Zel gave her the devil-in-a-white-dress smile. The one that guaranteed evil. "Are you sure?"

Ayaan looked at her—then at Shelia.

Shelia was sitting there trying to look innocent. However, when Ayaan tilted her head to get a true reaction, Shelia nodded. Then she stood up. "I knew you then, and I know you now. He was not surprised to see me. Was he the first person you told that I was back?"

"He's my best friend."

Shelia walked over and touched her on the arm. "Exactly."

Then Shelia walked over to Zel. "She's not the only one that needs a little self-reflection."

Zel looked at her. "What? I've moved on. I'm fucking now. No cobwebs."

"You're telling Ayaan to take off the dead carcass. I'm sure any man worth anything is put off by the smell of your dead carcass. I need you to set Barney Fife free."

"You told me to find someone."

"Right, and you did. Now you need someone that you don't forget to call when you're out of town."

Zel thought back. Crap, she hadn't called him. "Shit."

"Right."

Ayaan looked over at them. "You're all up in my business. Do I get to know what you're talking about?"

Shelia told the story of the death that brought them to Paris. Ayaan looked puzzled. "So two men died the same way, or were you two sharing?"

Shelia stopped. "It's complicated."

Ayaan looked at her. "Aren't we pouring our hearts out now?"

"Do you want me to start crying again?"

There wasn't anything in the world Ayaan wanted to know that would have her living through another bout of Shelia's tears. She turned to Zel. "So you stopped having sex since he died?"

"Yeah, something like that."

Ayaan looked at Zel as if she had grown another six feet. "It took you five years to find a rebound guy."

Zel wasn't ready to let that one slide. "Really? You're judging. How's your rebound guy?"

Ayaan shrugged. "He's great, as long as I keep fresh batteries around."

"Exactly."

"Now that I think about it, I already broke a few rebound guys. I do need to switch to human. They last longer. What's wrong with this Barney Fife guy?"

Zel closed her eyes. "Have you ever kissed someone and couldn't wait to get your clothes off? Or better yet, got wet at the thought of the anticipation? Or you can't even think when he kisses you. "

"Ummm. Well,"

"I know you have. I've seen that guy out there. Let's say my last collection was designed while I was flat on my back."

"Oh, damn. I'm with Shelia. Let Barney Fife go."

"I'm working on it."

Shelia shook her head. "No, don't work on it. Do it. Let him go. You're going to hurt him so cut the strings already. Damn."

Zel gave Shelia her best puppy dog eyes. "You sounded like me when you said that. I'm so proud."

"Whatever." Shelia hitched her head at Ayaan. "What about that six-foot-five guy that was shadow boxing with the plant?"

Ayaan's eyes started to twinkle. "Single dad. Don't know where the mom went. Full custody. His mother lives in another state. He's the sweetest."

Shelia squinted. "Barney Fife sweet."

"I really don't know. I've heard very tasty rumors. Mothers do talk, you know."

Zel tried a roadblock. "I live in Paris."

Shelia threw up her hands, "So does Barney Fife. While I loved your last line, I need you to upgrade. It doesn't have to be forever. I've seen Shadow Boxer's muscles flex. Can Fife scoop you up and flip you around? If he can't, he needs to go."

All three smiled at each other. Then a pall came over the room. They weren't friends. Not even close. Ayaan knew this was a short-lived camaraderie, and she had to ask the question she had been dreading for the last month and a half. "Are you going to try to take her?"

Shelia paused. It was no longer her right. "Legally, I can't."

Ayaan pursed her lips. "You could tell her who you are."

"Morally, I won't. She's so happy. She has such a gentle spirit."

Ayaan chuckled. "It's not what I would call it, but OK."

"I don't want to take away her security. That would be the worst thing I could possibly do. You're her mother. I chose you. I have to stand by my decision. You were the best choice. You still are."

Ayaan felt the tears falling down her face. "Crap. Now I'm pulling a Shelia."

Zel looked at Shelia concerned. "At what cost to you?"

"It doesn't matter the cost to me. As you reminded me, I'm a grown-ass woman. The only thing that matters is Kendall. I need to be stronger for Kendall. I can't go on like this, obviously."

Zel walked over and put her arms around Shelia.

Shelia extracted herself and walked away. "If you touch me, I'll cry—and I am really sick of crying." She turned to Ayaan. "She's yours. I'll live by that."

Ayaan thought for a moment, then said, "The adoption was open. I don't have the right to keep her completely away from you, but you did this all wrong. You should have given me some notice or something. You should have let me get used to the idea. I got selfish. I did. I know. I don't want anyone to take her away from me. I love her so much. We'll get some professional help in figuring this out. She is the most important thing."

Shelia thought about it. Ayaan was giving her a gift, a gift she didn't deserve. "Tell you what. Let me get my house in order, and then we'll figure it out."

Ayaan nodded.

Zel looked closely, "What does that mean?"

"I'm not leaving Devon. Stop asking. You know the sex you were just describing. Even though you can't imagine it, Devon blows me out of the water. It's amazing. You'd expect him to be Barney Fife, right? However, what that man can do with a bed is truly a gift. Hell, skip a bed. What he can do with a couch, loveseat, front and back seat of a car, shower. Girl. I'm not giving that up on a whim. I'm going to see what we can do together. If it doesn't work, it doesn't work." Shelia smiled. "But I'm going to need a little back time to figure that out."

"But you could be with anyone."

"No, I'm where I need to be. I know you don't understand. Half the time, I don't understand. I know you think I settled. So do I some days. Shit. I'm sure he thinks the same thing lately, but there is something there. We've ignored it far too long except—"

There was a gentle knock on the door.

When Ayaan opened it up, Kenneth was on the other side holding Kendall. "She told me she's not allowed to disturb you with the door closed, but since I'm an adult, I can."

"Kendall, sweetie, you know this is still disturbing."

"I know. I'm sorry Mommy, but it's not work time, it's my party. I thought it would be OK."

She looked so hopeful, Ayaan couldn't be mad at her. "Come here, birthday girl." She grabbed Kendall and tickled her a bit.

Kendall laughed. "Wait, why did Mr. Kenneth come get me instead of Cleo?"

"I like Mr. Kenneth. He's funny."

"You don't know Mr. Kenneth."

"Yes, I do. We played together. We're friends."

Without even looking at Shelia and Zel, she knew the look in their eyes was the same as earlier. She was tired of fighting. She was done fighting her frustration with Shelia. Shelia had said she was moving on. Ayaan believed her.

She was done fighting her ongoing attraction to Kenneth. She had been stronger the first time around before she knew what she was getting. All these years of forcibly keeping her distance had worn down her resolve. Damn, Zel was right. Her father was dead. Her family was right here. All she wanted to do now was wrap her arms around Kenneth's neck, breathe in his cologne, and bring him back to the place she denied him. He was in front of her watching all of this play on her face.

He always did read her expressions better than anyone else. He raised his eyebrows. He said, "You know, I always thought you needed time, space. I thought a month, maybe two, then maybe three. I didn't think five years. I bled every day."

She touched his forearm and kissed his cheek. This was between them, not Kendall, who no doubt was hanging onto every word, or Shelia or Zel. She felt their smug self-righteous eyes boring into her back. This was about Ayaan and Kenneth.

Ayaan heard Shelia and Zel shuffling in the background. Shelia said, "Listen, we'll leave you all alone."

With those words, Ayaan was released.

She looked into her daughter's eyes. "OK, Kendall baby, but seriously, this interruption is a one-time deal. Shake on it."

She shook hands with Kendall and then put her down. "Now, come on in. I want you to meet mommy's new friends."